SATAN'S KEYHOLE

A Western Duo

Les Savage, Jr.

CENTER POINT LARGE PRINT
THORNDIKE, MAINE

This Center Point Large Print edition
is published in the year 2018 by arrangement with
Golden West Literary Agency.

The text of this Large Print edition is unabridged.
In other aspects, this book may vary
from the original edition.

Set in 16-point Times New Roman type.

ISBN: 978-1-68324-695-4 (hardcover)
ISBN: 978-1-68324-699-2 (paperback)

Library of Congress Cataloging-in-Publication Data

Names: Savage, Les, author.
Title: Satan's keyhole : a Western duo / Les Savage, Jr.
Description: Center Point Large Print edition. | Thorndike, Maine :
    Center Point Large Print, 2017.
Identifiers: LCCN 2017051006| ISBN 9781683246954
    (hardcover : alk. paper) | ISBN 9781683246992 (pbk. : alk. paper)
Subjects: LCSH: Western stories. | Large type books.
Classification: LCC PS3569.A826 A6 2017 | DDC 813/.54—dc23
LC record available at https://lccn.loc.gov/2017051006

Printed and bound in Great Britain
by TJ International Ltd, Padstow, Cornwall

MIX
Paper from
responsible sources
FSC
www.fsc.org   FSC® C013056

SATAN'S KEYHOLE

A Western Duo

TABLE OF CONTENTS

Silver and Shells for General Kearny

I

The echoes of the shots were dead now, and the peons were crowding back into Santa Fe's moonlit San Francisco Street, looking after the four horsemen who galloped on down toward the plaza, driving Danny Macduff's mules in front of them. His left arm hanging useless, his right fist gripping his Remington .44, Macduff crouched, hidden in the shadowed *hacienda* doorway. Those four riders had galloped from beneath two of the hovels across the way with guns flaming at Macduff. He wondered bitterly who wanted him dead that badly, and what they expected to find in the pack saddles of his mangy mules.

Iron hasps creaked behind Macduff. He whirled to the opening door, Remington jerking up. He stopped his tightening finger just in time.

"*Señor* Riley?" said a woman's voice. "We didn't know if it was you they were shooting at. The peons are so stirred up. They have been firing their guns all night anyway. Come in quickly, please."

Patently she took him for someone else. But right now he would feel safer behind that solid oak door, and he had to get his wound tended. He stepped inside, and iron hasps creaked as the door closed.

11

"This way, *Señor* Riley," said the woman.

Macduff followed her toward a faint line of light that came from beneath another door at the end of the hall. She opened that door and stood by it, apparently wanting him to enter first. He stopped, too, momentarily to look at her.

Light spilled over blue-black hair piled up under a white *mantilla,* deep brown eyes that held his for a moment, scarlet lips, startling against the pallor of her face. She wore a *camisa*—the pleated white blouse of these *señoritas*—and a full silk skirt that trailed on the floor, revealing only the toes of her red slippers.

He looked past her to the inner *sala,* a large room, walls white-washed with *yeso,* barred windows set with semi-transparent mica. A *banco* ran all the way around, forming an adobe bench, covered with red blankets from Chimayo and fringed satins from Mexico City. There were four men.

The candles of the big center table lit only the front part of the room, and in the deep rear shadows stood two of the men, their faces mere blots in the darkness. The other two stood within the circle of light.

Macduff shot them a hard glance, then limped ahead into the *sala.* He stopped before the table, putting his gun away, cuffing his black felt hat from his long dark hair that curled down the back of his neck. The sun had burned his stubborn-

12

jawed face an Indian brown, but hadn't quite obliterated his Irish freckles.

"Did they hit your leg?" asked the woman, coming from behind.

Automatically Macduff glanced down at his leg. "No, that's an old one," he said wryly, then held out his left hand, sticky with the blood leaking down from his wound. "This is where they hit me . . . here."

"Sit down, please," she said, "and I'll have a *criada* bring some hot water and bandages."

She turned to call the servant, and before he had taken the chair by the table, a Navajo woman came through another doorway, the heavy silver-embroidered curtain rustling as she dropped it behind her. The *señorita* spoke softly in Spanish, and the *criada*, her face darkly impassive, bowed herself back through the curtain.

"Now, *Señor* Riley," said the woman, turning back, "I am *Señorita* Lajara Costillo." She indicated a hawk-faced young man, the silver-chased scabbard of his rapier showing beneath a blue, silk-lined riding cloak. "This," she said, "is *Don* Caspar Jamarillo."

He nodded curtly to Macduff, eyes narrowed.

"Look here," said Macduff, half rising. "We'd better get this straight. I'm not. . . ."

"Now, now," said the other man, stepping around the table and gently shoving Macduff back down. "We'll fix that wound before we do

13

the business. Incidentally I'm Doctor Leo Britt. Did you recognize who shot you?"

He was a pot-bellied, dowdy man in soiled fustian and rumpled waistcoat, black string tie hanging from a frayed choke collar. Yet, for all his sloppiness, there was something about his eyes. . . . He began taking off Macduff's shaggy old buffalo coat.

"I only got a good look at one of them before they high-tailed it with my mules," said Macduff. "He was a big tall *hombre* with long mustaches and Apache *botas*. . . ."

"Anton Chico," said Lajara Costillo heatedly. "That *maldito!*"

"Anton Chico?" asked Macduff.

"A bandit," explained the doctor, fishing out a Barlow knife and slitting Macduff's flannel shirt sleeve. "Though how he found out you'd be here tonight only the devil knows. That's an ugly wound, Riley. What you need is a drink. As the immortal bard says . . . 'Be large in mirth. . . .' "

" 'Anon, we'll drink the table round,' " Macduff finished the quotation almost automatically.

The doctor had reached for a silver jug of *pulque* on the table; he turned, jug and tumbler still held in his hands. "By Harry . . . an Irishman who quotes Shakespeare! It's rare one finds a gentleman of the old school in these god-forsaken mountains."

Macduff shrugged, almost sorry it had slipped

out. Then he turned, his eyes riveted to the man who had moved out of the shadows by the rear wall. Candlelight fell on broad shoulders and deep chest, an expensive tailed coat, pin-striped trousers, razor-creased, and polished Anson boots. Beneath a sweep of fair hair, clear blue eyes regarded Macduff candidly, but they held no hint of recognition.

"Mister Riley," said the man. "I trust you weren't indiscreet enough to carry the money on those mules."

For just that moment, Danny Macduff was caught off guard, and his mouth opened in stunned surprise. Then his dark face became carefully blank, and his mouth snapped shut. He looked at his tall, fair brother with veiled eyes, thinking: *All right, Terrance Macduff, if that's the way you want it, all right!*

But the others had caught that unguarded moment, and the woman was watching Danny closely, a new speculation in her glance. The little lights that came and went in *Don* Jamarillo's eyes might have been a trick of the flickering candle, or a new, growing suspicion. Dr. Leo Britt took a step forward and leaned toward Danny, his voice ironic.

"The man who asked you the question is Mister Coe, the agent for Klierman Shippers, here in Santa Fe. He is, let me assure you, one of us."

"Oh," said Danny. "Mister Coe. Well, Mister

15

Coe, I didn't carry any money on my mules, if that makes you feel better."

The last time Danny had seen his brother, Terrance had been stationed at Leavenworth, the blue coat with the brass buttons of the United States Cavalry over his big chest instead of these expensively tailored civilian clothes. It struck Danny Macduff that he had stepped into something deep here, and that he might very well be in over his head right now.

The Navajo *criada* had come back with a big jar of hot water and strips of clean white cotton. The doctor peeled Danny's split sleeve away from the wound and swabbed it clean.

"Perhaps," he said, "you would like to tell us where the money is, then, Mister Riley. We haven't much time."

Jamarillo shoved his cloak back and let one hand slide to the hilt of his sword, leaning forward a little, eyes glittering. The woman shifted impatiently, pulling her *mantilla* tighter. The doctor finished bandaging Danny's arm, stood up.

"Well, Mister Riley . . . ?"

Whatever Danny would have answered was stopped by the muted thud of hoofs from the street outside, the creak of men swinging down from saddles. Dr. Britt turned.

"That might be our good Captain Antonito Valdez coming after the money, and, then again, it might not."

Lajara Costillo snatched up Macduff's buffalo coat, helping him out of the chair. "You'd better get in the other room till we make sure. And you, too, *Señor* Coe. Conchita, get rid of this stuff, *pronto*."

The *criada* collected the jar and soiled cotton padding from the *sala*. Britt disappeared into the shadowed hall, going to the front door as *Señorita* Costillo herded Danny and his tall brother into a darkened room. Danny slipped his buffalo coat on, turning to his brother.

"That was a fine greeting you gave me out there, after four years," he said.

"I didn't think you wanted to be given away . . . Mister Riley," said Terrance.

"I thought it was *you* who didn't want to be given away . . . Mister Coe," said Danny. "What is this, Terrance? Who's Riley? And why did that *bandido* expect me to carry money on my mules?"

Terrance spoke very carefully. "Wait a minute . . . you mean to tell me you're not going under the name of Riley?"

"No, dammit, no! I'm Danny Macduff, and I'll always be Danny Macduff. I've been up north, hunter for Bent's Fort. Bent paid me a year's wages in beaver plews and I was coming down here to cash them in. If that Anton Chico expected to find any money on my mules, he'll get a mighty big surprise."

Terrance laughed wryly. "You can bet he will. They expected to find thirty thousand dollars in silver on your mules."

Danny grabbed his arm. "Tell me what it's about, Terrance."

"Ease up on my arm and I will," said the other. "If you've been north, you wouldn't know the United States declared war on Mexico in May, Eighteen Forty-Six. New Mexico's a northern province of Mexico and it rates a first-class attack. General Stephen Kearny is approaching Las Vegas right now with the Army of the West. As soon as he takes Las Vegas, he'll move on Santa Fe."

Danny let a low whistle through his teeth. "War . . . no wonder the peons were raising such a ruckus outside. But how come you're here in civvies, instead of out there with Kearny, where you belong?"

"The War Department had been preparing for this ever since the Texas trouble," said Terrance. "I'd been riding escort on the wagon trains over the Santa Fe Trail, knew this country, spoke the language. We always stopped at Chouteau's Island and let the wagons come on to Santa Fe, then picked them up on the return trip, so I wasn't known here in the town.

"Last January I was transferred from the Cavalry to Intelligence and planted in Santa Fe as Mister Coe, agent for Klierman Shippers, a

18

Yankee outfit with a branch at this end. My job is to do all I can to aid our troop movements, and to try and stop any conspiracies that will work against us. And this thing you've stepped into, my boy, is a conspiracy to end all conspiracies."

He stopped a moment, listening to the muted hubbub of talk at the outer door. Dr. Britt seemed to be arguing with someone. Then Terrance turned back to Danny.

"Marching into Santa Fe, Kearny will have to take Glorieta Pass and Apache Pass through the Sangre de Cristos. Either of those cañons holds a dozen spots perfect for ambush. Manuel Armijo, the governor here, and also general of the Mexican army, is an unscrupulous, conniving despot who'd sell out his own mother for a few *pesos*. His tyranny has created a host of enemies for him in Santa Fe. They'd do anything to get Armijo out. I put it into their hands to offer him money to withdraw his troops, and to abdicate."

"That's the money that was to be brought by Riley?"

Terrance nodded. "Armijo must have realized what a powder keg he was sitting on. He agreed to sell out for thirty thousand dollars. This James Riley isn't known here in Santa Fe. None of us have ever seen him. But we were given his description by partisans who chose him for the job. He was in Las Vegas collecting the last of

19

the money, was due here tonight at seven, with the whole sum."

"And if Armijo doesn't get that money?"

"General Kearny and his whole command," finished Terrance, "will ride into an ambush somewhere between here and Las Vegas, and will stand a good chance of being wiped out."

He turned toward the door suddenly. Boots thudded down the front hallway and into the main *sala*. There was the muted clank of accouterments, and a young, arrogant voice said in Spanish:

"*Buenas noches, Señorita* Costillo . . . *Don* Jamarillo. Governor Armijo grows impatient. It is past the time when the money was due at the *palacio*. He sent me after it."

"Captain Valdez," Terrance whispered to Danny. "Mexican dragoons. Tough *hombre* to meet in a scrap."

Valdez's voice sounded again, sharp with rising anger. "*Por supuesto*, Doctor Britt, you told me *Señor* Riley had not yet arrived. But you forgot to wipe the blood off his chair. Are you trying to hide him from me? *Cabo*, take that door . . . I'll take this one!"

Before he had finished the order to his corporal, his steps sounded swiftly toward the curtained doorway to the room in which the two brothers stood. Already Danny was forcing Terrance to the big chest that stood on the far side.

"Let go," hissed Terrance. "This is my business."

"Don't be a damn' fool," snapped Danny, shoving him down between the wall and the chest. "You know what they do to spies as well as I do. If they got suspicious about you being here with me, it'd be the firing squad."

Then he was taking a swift step toward the door, digging into his buffalo coat to get at his Remington. The curtain was yanked aside with a tinkling clash of silver, and Macduff stopped with his gun half drawn.

Captain Antonito Valdez stood there with one hand holding the curtain back, the other gripping a big Walker Colt.

"Ah," he said. "*Señor* Riley. Won't you please come out."

Danny Macduff stepped through the door and the captain moved aside to let him pass. He was a rakish young dragoon, Captain Valdez, a tight cuirass of double-folded deerskin worn beneath his blue jacket with its red cuffs and collar; his eyes had a flash and an arrogance that matched his voice.

"Why did you hide him, Doctor?" he asked. "I thought we were all *compadres* in this."

"I wasn't sure it was you," said Dr. Britt blandly. "Anton Chico has already made his appearance tonight. If he knows, aren't the others just as likely to know?"

21

"You brought the money?" Valdez asked Macduff.

"Apparently," said the doctor, "he didn't. Chico jumped him outside and ran off with Mister Riley's mules. But Mister Riley said he didn't have the money on them. And Mister Riley hasn't yet told us where he did have it."

Valdez looked at Macduff, face hardening. "You will tell me, señor, where it is."

Terrance was out of it now, and Danny knew he should have told them long ago who he really was.

"I think you ought to know," he said, "that I'm not James Riley. I'm a hunter for Bent's Fort. The name's Macduff . . . Danny Macduff."

Valdez's eyes widened. He looked from the doctor to the girl, then back to Maduff, his surprise clouded by anger. Lajara Costillo made a small, unbelieving gesture.

"Señor, this is no time for joking, I assure you."

"I don't think so, either," Danny told her. "That's why I'm not joking."

Dr. Britt leaned forward, and his eyes suddenly held a dangerous flame.

"I always thought thirty thousand dollars was a lot to trust with a man we'd never seen," he said. "And he chooses Macduff, of all names."

"Perhaps we'd better take him to the *palacio*," said Valdez. "Governor Armijo has a way of dealing with such as *Señor* Riley."

"Macduff is the name," said Danny. "Macduff. And I'm not going to any *palacio*. This isn't any of my business."

The two dragoons who had come in with the captain moved toward Danny from the side. *Don Jamarillo* stepped around the table.

Danny took a jerky step toward Valdez, bending forward almost unconsciously, hand taut above his gun. Valdez curled a thumb around the hammer of his Walker, cocking it. Danny hung there for a moment, almost mad enough to go for his gun anyway. . . .

There had been two men standing in the gloom at the rear of the room when Macduff had first come into the house. One had been his brother Terrance. The other was still there. Now that man moved forward. The light suddenly caught his face, beetling brows over jet black eyes that flicked from Valdez to Britt to Macduff, and finally to the *señorita*. Still with his hand clawed out over his Remington, Macduff caught the almost imperceptible movement that might have been the man's hand dipping for his gun.

Then the *señorita* gave the man a quick, hard look, and he subsided back into the shadows. Almost at the same time, she stepped forward and caught Macduff's good arm.

"Don't be a fool," she said hotly.

Valdez smiled thinly. "I almost believe you'd do it, *Señor* Riley."

Eyes on the black bore of that Walker Colt, Macduff finally let the whole knotty tension slip from his body. Valdez indicated the Irishman was to precede him into the hall. Macduff limped forward, and the shadows in the hallway reached out for him, falling darkly across his square, broad shoulders.

II

New Mexico, as a northern province of Mexico, had bowed for ten years under the heavy, despotic hand of the fabulous Governor Manuel Armijo. Standing before him now, in the executive office at the governor's palace, Macduff could well believe all the bizarre tales he'd heard of the man.

Armijo was mountainous behind his great, ornate desk, his tight *charro* jacket strained to the bursting point by his tremendous torso, hands thick-fingered and fat beneath the flowing sleeves of his white silk shirt. But it was the eyes that marked the man. The heavy, narrowed lids couldn't veil the craft and ruthless intelligence it must have taken to build such an intricate, despotic empire out of this barren province. Macduff sensed that the great, fat Armijo could play a dozen different parts, as the occasion demanded, and that right now he was playing the suave, magnanimous governor up to the hilt. "My *palacio* is yours, *Señor* Riley." Armijo smiled. "Sit down, please. Have a *puro*?"

Macduff declined the cigar, and took a carved oak chair in front of the desk. Living among the Indians up at Bent's Fort, he had learned to see things without actually seeming to. And though his eyes never left Armijo, he had taken in the whole room.

Hung on the walls were festoons of Apache's ears, collected by Armijo in reprisal for the Indians' scalping of Mexicans. Beneath the strings of ears were ancient spears and rusty cuirasses that must have dated back to De Vargas. Black Bayeta blankets and red Chimayos were draped over the usual *banco* running all the way around the room, and upon one sat the dowdy, smiling Dr. Britt.

Valdez stood very close to MacDuff. He had taken the Irishman's Remington; it lay on the desk before Armijo. There were two guards by the open door, one inside, one outside in the hall, both armed with the huge, smooth-bore *escopetas* of the Mexican dragoon.

Armijo took one of his own *puros*, bit off the end, took his own time lighting it. His chair squeaked as he eased his prodigious bulk back in it.

"I'm disappointed in you, *Señor* Riley," he said heavily. "I made a bargain with your go-betweens, was very specific about how it was to be carried out. In the first place, my name wasn't to be mentioned . . . I wasn't to appear in it till the money finally reached me. You must realize what would happen if the people of Santa Fe realized I was . . ."

"Selling them out?" Macduff supplied.

Armijo flushed. "*Señor* . . . please!"

"That's what it amounts to." Macduff shrugged. "You get paid for withdrawing your troops and throwing over your office. Why not put it plainly?"

"This is intrigue, *señor* . . . one never puts things plainly in intrigue," growled the governor. "However, you don't seem to realize that every minute you spend in Santa Fe is another minute in which a dozen different factions will try their best to kill you. You saw how Anton Chico was willing to murder you for that money. He and his *bandidos* form only one party. There are the common soldiers. They would tear you to pieces if they knew you brought the money that would mean the *Americanos* march into Santa Fe without a shot. And the peons . . ."

"And the Farrerra party," said Britt.

Armijo's face darkened. "*Sí*. They are the strongest of all . . . minor politicians who have become fat under my rule. They would stand to lose everything if I . . . ah . . . abdicated. They would stop at nothing to keep the money from reaching me. Their nominal leader is the emigration officer appointed from Mexico, Carlos Farrerra. But behind him stands another, an unknown, whose backing makes them more powerful and more dangerous than any of the other factions. Now, *Señor* Riley, you must see how stupid it would be to continue this farce. Surely your life is worth more than a paltry thirty thousand dollars. . . ."

Anger again flared inside Macduff. He gripped the carved arms of the chair till his knuckles showed white.

"I'm *not* Riley. Why won't you believe that?"

Armijo sighed heavily. "We were given Riley's description. Irish, obviously . . . short and broad-shouldered with brown hair and brown eyes, in this country long enough to be darkened by the sun. . . ."

"All of which might fit five out of ten Irishmen," snapped Macduff.

"And of course," said Armijo, "it was just by chance that you came down the *entrada* at the time *Señor* Riley was due, and just by chance you chose the *señorita*'s doorway."

"They were waiting for Riley just opposite," said Macduff. "There wasn't another place to hide within a hundred yards."

Armijo leaned forward, his voice catching with impatience. "*Señor*, were you fool enough to think you could begin conspiring also, to think you could play one side off against the other and maybe be left with the money yourself?"

" 'Now, whether he kill Cassio,' " quoted the doctor with a chuckle, " 'or Cassio kill him, or each do kill the other, every way makes my gain.' "

Armijo cast a glance at Britt. "*Sí*, doctor, that is it. *Pues*, it seems our *Señor* Riley wasn't cut out for intrigue. There are right times to play that kind of a game. And wrong times."

Macduff stood suddenly. Valdez made a swift, instinctive move toward his gun, then stopped like that, waiting.

"Let's quit fencing," flamed the Irishman. "I'm fed up. I'm not Riley and I don't know where the hell your filthy bribe is. That's all I've got to say, whether you believe it or not!"

Armijo's eyes took on a cruel glitter. "*Pues*, there is always La Garita."

"La Garita?"

"Yes," explained Dr. Britt softly. "It's the old Spanish prison behind the *palacio*. Whenever a man disappears suddenly, here in Santa Fe, it's rumored that a questioning party might find him in La Garita . . . if the party was fool enough to question."

Macduff saw it was the end of the rope. He took a slow breath, setting himself. The doctor had no obvious weapon, though he might carry a gun beneath his coat. Armijo could reach the

Remington lying on the desk, but Macduff felt sure he could move a little faster. Valdez, then, was the man, his big bone-butted Walker riding high out of his hand-tooled holster.

Armijo's voice was sly. "There are some marvelous implements in La Garita . . . left there from the Inquisition. My *hombres* have become artists in their use. Persuasion, you know, *Señor* Riley. . . ."

The desk was slantwise across one corner of the room, and the way Macduff stood, the doorway was within his line of vision. An awareness of the dragoon standing outside the door had been growing on Macduff ever since he had risen from the chair. Macduff turned imperceptibly, and caught the man's face, the beetling brows over beady eyes.

The last time Danny Macduff had seen that man, he had stood in the shadows at the rear of the main *sala* in *Señorita* Costillo's *hacienda*, and he hadn't worn any dragoon's uniform then. The hope of it almost hurt Macduff. He knew whatever he did here by the desk would be useless because of those two guards. But if one of them was the *señorita*'s man, if she had sent him. . . . It was the chance Macduff would have to take, and he gathered himself for it. Then the doctor came forward, leaning his hands on the desk. The twinkle had gone from his little blue eyes, and his soft voice held a strange menace.

Macduff suddenly realized that the doctor might be more than just a chuckling pot-gut who spouted Shakespeare.

"Now, Riley," said the doctor. "We've given you your choice. Tell us where the money is, or . . . La Garita."

Perhaps they didn't expect a lame man to move quite so fast. Macduff's eyes were still on the doctor when he threw himself aside in a sudden, lurching movement toward Valdez.

With the Irishman's shoulder in his middle, Valdez let out an explosive wheeze, reeled back, hand grabbing for his Walker. But Macduff already had both his hands on the gun. They slammed against the *banco*, rolled off, pulling a Chimayo blanket with them. Macduff hit the floor with Valdez on top of him, and had the Walker out, jerking it to bear on the doctor and Armijo from beneath the captain's body.

The huge governor had risen, one fat hand outflung for Macduff's .44 where it lay on the desk. He stopped that hand just above the gun, heavy-lidded eyes still wide with surprise.

The doctor had taken his hands off the desk. One of them was sliding back out of his coat where he had reached for something a little too late.

"I thought maybe you were heeled, Doc," said Macduff.

" 'Why should I play the Roman fool and die

on my own sword?' " quoted Britt, forcing a chuckle.

"Get off, Valdez," said the Irishman. "And do it right, unless you want one of your own slugs through your brisket." The young captain rose carefully, face dark with rage and shame. The guard who had stood inside the door was sprawled on the floor where *Señorita* Costillo's man had knocked him with the butt of his *escopeta*.

Macduff began backing toward the door, glad he had taken that chance.

"You're a fool," Dr. Britt said. "There are a hundred soldiers between you and the outside. And if you do escape, there are a dozen different factions that'll be hunting your hide. . . ."

Macduff slammed the door on his words. The big hulking man outside grabbed his shoulder, turned him toward the rear of the palace.

"I'm Ancho," he said. "The *señorita* is waiting in the Arroyo Mascaros with horses."

He was peeling off the blue dragoon's coat. Beneath it were his two six-guns, belt buckled up tight around his thick waist so the holsters wouldn't show beneath the bottom of the coat. As they reached the turn in the corridor, Armijo's voice rang down the hall after them like angry thunder.

"*Capitán del Guardia*, call out the guard! The Yankee has escaped. *Capitán del Guardia!*"

Macduff and Ancho were already pounding around the turn when from ahead came the sound of the dragoons running. From a barrack room, dark figures lurched into the hall. A gun blared. Lead ricocheted off the wall, chipping adobe into Macduff's face.

Ancho dug high heels into the earthen floor, trying to stop. His twin sixes were already out. One of the dragoons charging down the hall suddenly pitched forward with a scream. Another tipped over sideways, still running, hit the wall, and slid down, finally rolling to a stop. The Captain of the Guard tripped over his body and fell, bullets from his gun plowing the floor.

Macduff yanked Ancho back around the turn. But already from behind them came the pound of other feet—Britt and Armijo and Valdez.

The Irishman spotted a square blot across the hall, and both he and Ancho jumped toward it, shoving open the door and lurching into the dark room just as the remaining dragoons came around the turn. A soldier tried to follow them in through the door. Valdez's Walker felt heavy and unfamiliar in Macduff's hand, but his first shot caught that man in the door, spilling him over backward into the hall.

Outside they could hear the Captain of the Guard calling: "We have them trapped in that *sala*, Governor!"

"Well, go in and get them!" roared Armijo.

Backing farther into the room, Macduff brought the smoking Walker up again. He didn't know how many there were. It didn't matter much. They had made a good try, anyway.

But the body of the dragoon Macduff had shot was lying half in, half out the door, and it must have discouraged those outside. Now that the action was over, he could feel the insistently throbbing pain in his wounded left arm. Ancho was fumbling with something behind Macduff.

"*Dios*," he muttered. "There's a door here, but it's locked."

Macduff stumbled around a big table, lurched up against the solid sweating body of the man. He felt for the door handle, found it, an ancient relic of hammered silver.

"Get away," he said. "I'll try to shoot the lock apart."

His shots were deafening, echoing out into the hall. With acrid powder smoke choking him, he heaved against the ironbound door. It gave, hurling him into another dark room. Ancho followed behind, and over his lumbering footsteps Macduff heard Armijo's raging voice.

"Go in after them, you *borrachónes*! What kind of coyote soldiers do you call yourselves?"

There was a sudden rush. The thunder of gunfire rolled inside. Then there was a moment of silence as the dragoons must have realized they had rushed an empty room. Macduff found another door in the dark, unlocked. It led into the corridor beyond the turn. Their feet made a muted thud on the earth, past the deserted barrack room, to the end of the hall.

The apartments behind the Palace of the Governors had been built in an earlier century, to house the dignitaries of the Spanish government. Now they were officers' quarters, adobe houses grouped around flagstone courtyards with green willows sighing above bright-roofed wells. Hugging the shadowed gloom of an adobe wall, Ancho led through the first *placita* to an iron-grilled gateway. The sound of pursuit was becoming audible behind them as they reached the main gate.

Macduff saw where Ancho had gotten the uniform, then. In the shadows of the wall lay the guard, stripped to the white pantaloons dragoons wore beneath their blue trousers. The iron grille complained rustily as Ancho shoved it open, poking his black head out carefully, looking up and down the street.

Across the way was a row of mud-walled hovels. Between two of these Ancho led Macduff, rounding a crude piñon hayrack. Somewhere a baby cried plaintively. A burro grumbled on its tether behind the houses. A narrow winding alleyway led finally to the Arroyo Mascaros.

They half slid, half ran down its steep bank, feet plunging into the shallow water at the bottom. A fringe of cottonwoods bulked across the stream, and Ancho pushed through the underbrush. Macduff followed, thorns catching at his shaggy buffalo coat, scraping across his elkhide leggings. In a clearing stood four horses, held by a *criado* in white trousers and shirt. The girl had changed to a split Crow riding skirt, and was muffled to the chin in a dark cloak, a black felt hat with a wide soft brim taking the place of her *mantilla*.

She turned nervously as the two men broke through the agrito. "Ancho?"

"*Sí, señorita*," said Ancho. "It was easy."

She was only half listening. Her eyes, shadowed beneath the hat brim, were on Macduff.

"Why send Ancho after me?" he asked. "I thought you were with the doctor."

"Doctor Britt still thinks you are *Señor* Riley," she said. "But after you left, Ancho told me about you . . . El Cojo!"

A fleeting grin caught at Macduff's mouth in the gloom. El Cojo—The Lame One. The Apaches had tacked that on him up around Bent's Fort.

"How did Ancho know? I never got this far south."

"Ancho is part Apache," she said. "They have sort of a grapevine, the Indians. I imagine you're known to every Apache from the territories to Mexico. It's a real compliment to have

35

them admit a white man can out-track them."

He shrugged. "I was a hunter. Tracking was just part of my business."

"You may not be Riley," she said. "But if you're as good as Ancho said, you're about the only man in Santa Fe who can save Kearny from that ambush."

He turned sharply to her, but Ancho's voice stopped him. "*Señorita*, the dragoons!"

III

For a long time they stayed there in the thicket, holding the horses, waiting. Valdez appeared at the top of the arroyo periodically, rode parallel to it for a block, then turned up another street. The girl moved closer to Macduff, and the scent of her hair made him shift uneasily.

"How do you fit in with this thing?" he asked.

"From the very first, the *ricos* . . . the land-owners . . . have opposed Governor Armijo," she said. "My father led their party, and it became known as the Costillo faction. We tried every way to force Armijo out, but he was too strong. Two years ago my father disappeared. . . ."

"La Garita?"

Her face paled. "Probably. That's where Armijo puts most of his political enemies. Since then I have led the Costillos."

"If you're so bitterly against Armijo, why try so hard to see that he gets this money?" asked Macduff.

"Only to get rid of him, don't you see?" she said hotly. "Anything to get him out . . . *anything!* He is such a despot, so cruel, so greedy. He's taxed us heavily, yet almost every landowner north of Socorro put money into that fund of thirty thousand. With all the Farrerras and their spies in Santa Fe, and Anton Chico, and all the other parties who would stand to lose if Armijo abdicated, we couldn't collect the money here. We chose Las Vegas. And when the thirty thousand was gathered, our partisans there were to choose a man who could get through with the silver. The Costillos know how little chance they stand of removing Armijo by force . . . we tried it a couple of times before. But if that money doesn't reach him, we're desperate enough to try it again, to storm the *palacio* and take him ourselves."

"Doctor Britt . . . is he with you, or Armijo?"

"He was the go-between for Armijo," she said. "On the surface, he's just a harmless little man Armijo keeps around to doctor his gout and to amuse him. But I've heard it whispered that Britt is master of Armijo when it comes to intrigue, that he has just as many irons in the fire as the governor."

"Valdez?"

She shrugged, smiling faintly. "About the only honest man in Santa Fe. A blind, hot-headed young fool who would die for Armijo. He and a few other trusted dragoons are the only soldiers who know of this thing. Naturally, if the rest of the army found they were being sold out, they'd revolt. The same with the peons. No telling what would happen to Armijo then."

"Now," he said, "that we have all the other characters in their proper places, we come to me. You said I was the only man who could save Kearny. . . ."

"Something has happened to Riley, obviously," she said. "He was due at my *hacienda* five or six hours ago. Apparently he has been intercepted somewhere between Santa Fe and Las Vegas. The fact that Anton Chico was waiting for him opposite my doorway proves the secret leaked out. A good tracker, working backward on the trail from here to Las Vegas, would stand a chance of finding Riley's sign, and trailing from there. . . ."

"But why me? You must know a hundred Indians who could do it."

"The only Indians I would trust are my servants, and they can't track like you. Ancho himself told me that."

"Everybody thinks I'm Riley," he said. "Here's a *bandido* and his killers after my hair because they want the money. Armijo's after my ears

38

because he thinks I'm playing both ends against the middle, and because he wants the money. A man nobody knows leading a bunch of small-time politicians who don't want the money to reach Armijo, and who, incidentally, want the money themselves. Every peon in Santa Fe set to murder me if they find out about the plot. The whole Mexican army in between here and Las Vegas. I'd be a fine fool, wouldn't I, to go wandering down the Pecos Trail to Las Vegas . . . like a fool hen sitting on a branch, waiting for every chicken hawk in the Sangre de Cristos to jump it."

"*Sí, señor,*" she said. "But sometimes it takes just that kind of a fine fool to save an army, or a nation, or a people. I thought perhaps you were he."

He looked down at her, a grin catching at his mouth. There were other issues involved, of course. There was Kearny's Army of the West that would stand a chance of being wiped out. There was Terrance, whose mission would fail, and who would probably be discovered and stood up against the wall. There was even James Riley, who, by all the Irish in him, Danny would have helped. Any of those things were enough for Macduff. Yet, somehow, they didn't mean as much as the woman, standing there with the scent of her blue-black hair disturbing him, her eyes shining up at him, asking him to do it.

"You thought right," he said. "I'm just exactly that kind of fool."

• • •

It was long past midnight, and only a few peons lurched drunkenly homeward down the entrance of the Santa Fe Trail into San Francisco Street. Bordering the road on one side was a line of hovels, and on the other two walled *haciendas*, one of them *Señorita* Costillo's. Macduff and the others had waited there in the arroyo until Valdez had ceased searching the city for them, then had wound through narrow back alleys and streets in the poorer section of town, finally nearing the woman's house. Halting in the shadow of a vine-covered wall while Ancho scouted ahead, Macduff leaned forward to tighten the nose band on his gelding.

"Isn't it dangerous going back to the *hacienda* this way?" he asked. "If anyone in Armijo's office recognized Ancho, they'd know where I would go."

"Ancho was careful not to be recognized," said Lajara Costillo. "And the servants wouldn't allow anyone in but those who have been working with us."

Still, Macduff felt the skin crawl along the back of his neck as they rode along the wall and through the entrance that led into the *placita*. The girl swung gracefully from her skittish little palomino, calling for a servant.

"Where is that Pepe?" she said impatiently. "Ancho, is he drunk again?"

Ancho shrugged. "Probably, *señorita*. I will have another *criado* attend to the horses as soon as we are inside."

The girl dropped her reins and followed Ancho toward the house, and Macduff took up the rear. He didn't know exactly why, but as he moved into the gloom beneath the arcade down one side of the *placita*, his hand slipped down to the bone butt of Captain Valdez's Walker Colt. The woman's skirts rustled through the door into the main *sala* ahead of Macduff, and her voice sounded strained.

"*Caracoles*, have they all gone to bed? Conchita, you lazy *Indio*, will you bring some light. . . ."

"That's quite all right," said a sardonic voice. "I don't mind the dark at all."

Before the voice had finished, Ancho gave a sick grunt. Macduff threw himself forward with some wild thought of protecting the woman, his gun coming out even as Ancho's heavy body hit the floor. The Irishman's finger was tightening on his trigger, his arm raising to throw down on the blot of scuffling figures ahead of him. Then he realized he might hit *Señorita* Costillo. She gave a terrified scream that was cut off sharply.

A man lurched in between Macduff and the sound of her voice. Sensing a blow, Macduff ducked in, hard and fast. Instead of the man's gun hitting Macduff's head, the man's elbow hit his shoulder.

Macduff lunged up, pistol-whipping the unseen face above him. He heard a sharp cry. Then the man was gone from in front of him, and he was stumbling over a body that must have been Ancho. He would have gone flat, but his hand found the big center table, pain burning through him as he put his weight suddenly on his wounded left arm.

The front door slammed open. On his knees by the table, Macduff saw three figures silhouetted in the door. Two men went through first, a struggling shape between them that was the girl, head covered by the blanket. Then the last man followed them out, running.

Macduff lurched after them. Before he reached the outer door, he heard the creak of saddles, the clatter of horses breaking into a gallop. Then he was out in the street, still not daring to shoot after them, because one rider carried the woman across the withers of his mount, head on one side, kicking feet on the other.

Hopelessly he watched the swiftly receding figures disappear down the *entrada* and onto the Santa Fe Trail. One of the men turned, and a strange wild laugh pealed back to Macduff, mocking him.

He turned finally, realizing that many peons were in the street, brought by the noise. They were moving toward him in little knots. None of them had slept off their Taos lightning and their brandy. Their faces were sullen and ugly. Macduff began backing toward the door of the *hacienda*.

"¡*Hola!*" shouted a big Mexican with mustaches a foot long. "An *Americano, compadres* . . . a *gringo!*"

Another dressed in flapping white trousers laughed nastily. "Maybe he doesn't know there's a war on, Pedro. Maybe we better let him know."

"*Sí*," laughed Pedro, yanking a gleaming machete from his red sash. "Cut off his ears to hang on the governor's walls."

The butt of Macduff's gun was sticky with perspiration. They were closing in, and others were drawing dirks, and one or two carried *escopetas*. Macduff's foot hit a rock and he stumbled a little.

Pedro laughed, drawing back his machete. Macduff had seen that kind of throw before, but he took another step, waiting, knowing what his shot would start.

Pedro's machete was behind his head. A man brought up his *escopeta*. Someone shouted.

With that shining machete for a target, Macduff fired, throwing himself backward. Lead ricocheted from steel with a scream, and the Mexican's howl was drowned by the swift pound of feet as the others broke forward. The man

43

with the *escopeta* fired, but Macduff was already rolling through the door, and the lead plunked into adobe a foot above his head. Running forward, another peon brought his *escopeta* flat against his belly for a spot shot.

Macduff's second slug caught him in the chest. He dropped his *escopeta* and slammed into the wall before he could stop himself, then slid to the ground, clutching at his chest. Macduff was inside the door then, scrambling to his feet, slamming it shut and shooting the bolt.

He could hear them milling around outside, cursing and talking in swift, angry Spanish. But even the excitement of war wasn't as strong as the century-old traditions that held them from breaking into the *hacienda*.

Macduff turned, feeling his way along the pitch-black hall and into the main *sala*. There were still some coals gleaming faintly from the stove that stood in one corner of the room. He hunted for the silver tongs, and fished out one of the live coals. Holding it with the tongs, he stepped over Ancho's body to the table, lighting a candle.

Ancho lay sprawled by the table, stabbed, dead.

Then, the flaring light revealed the other man, over against the *banco*. One big hand was at his chest, dark blue fustian coat drawn up into little folds by his clutching fingers. Macduff's face went dead white beneath its tan.

"Terrance!"

Terrance opened his eyes, looking at Danny a long time before he seemed to see him. Blood frothed from his lips when he spoke.

"Waited . . . waited in the other room till you left with the captain, Danny. Was going to help the *señorita* get you from the palace. She said to stay here and wait for Riley. I had to, Danny. . . ."

"I know," said Danny huskily, trying to help him up.

"No," choked Terrance Macduff. "No, Danny. I'm done. *Don* Jamarillo must have been a Farrerra all along. Planted in the Costillo party."

"Jamarillo?"

"Remember the hawk-faced gent . . . ? Blue riding cloak and sword, here with the doc when you first came? He put his blade through me from behind, after the *señorita* left with Ancho. Then he took care of the servants, let those other *hombres* in when they came. Farrerra came, too. He's not the real leader, though . . . just a stooge. . . ."

He coughed weakly. Danny tried to say something, but Terrance waved it aside.

"It's your job, now, Danny," he gasped. "They must've thought I was dead. Left me lying here. I learned who's really behind the Farrerras. He's the one you have to get, Danny. Armijo doesn't compare with him, or Anton Chico. He's the most dangerous . . . Your job, Danny . . . It's up to you now."

Danny grasped his shoulders as he trailed off, almost shouting: "Terrance, who is he? Terrance . . . ?"

Then he stopped shouting, because Terrance Macduff was dead.

He kneeled a long time beside his brother, looking at the wall without actually seeing it, his dark face hard and bleak.

IV

Centuries before, when the first Spaniards had come north from Mexico and had seen the mountains east of Santa Fe, lifting their crimson spires above the valley, they had called them Montes del Sangre de Cristo—Mountains of the Blood of Christ. Two passes, Apache and Glorieta, formed the gateway through the Sangre de Cristos to Santa Fe. Riding along the trail of the horsemen who had carried off Lajara Costillo, Macduff reached Apache Pass an hour after the sun had risen.

Behind the stables, Macduff had found the man who might have been Pepe, only he wasn't drunk; he was dead. Jamarillo had finished off the other male servants, too, and had tied the *criadas* in their quarters.

After Macduff had released them and waited for their hysterical sobbing to cease, they had helped him stuff tortillas and maize in the beaded saddlebags on the gelding. Slipping out the rear way, he had been on the trail less than an hour after the horsemen had ridden away down the *entrada* with Lajara.

That's how it was in his mind now. No longer the formality of *Señorita* Costillo, but just Lajara. The way a man thought of a woman when he'd known her for a long time, or when he suddenly realized how much she meant to him.

The trail, for Macduff, was like the pages of a book, every mark was a word that told him of the men he was following. He knew that one of the riders must be an Indian because one of the horses was unshod, and that the woman was still being carried across a horse's withers, because the front hoofs of one animal were sinking in deeper than its hind hoofs.

At midmorning he had gone through Apache Pass, and was entering Glorieta Pass. He saw that the riders had passed through there ahead of him shortly before dawn, for the dew had dried in their tracks.

Live grass began to rise immediately after being trodden on, and rose for three days afterward until it was straight again. When Macduff crossed a glade of short green grama, he dismounted and studied it, able to tell just how many hours ago the hoofs of horses had crushed it.

Finally the trail cut up the side of the pass into dark stands of piñon and cedar. Up on the slope that way, Macduff got a view down the pass. A quarter mile ahead was a vedette of Mexican dragoons, red cuffs and collars gay in the sun, accouterments glittering, horses ground-hitched.

Farther on, dust hung over the cañon in a dim yellow plume. That was Armijo's main army then, and Glorieta Pass was where he planned to ambush Kearny. It was a good position, not a very long line to hold with the slopes rising steeply on either side. It wouldn't be hard to hide in the thick timber on each slope, letting Kearny's skirmishers and scouts filter through, then come down on the main force of Americans.

Kearny didn't know the country, and his Army of the West would be weary and sick from the hellish march across the Jornada del Muerto. Armijo would have everything just about all his own way.

The pines formed a heavy forest that let the sun through now and then in dappled patterns, and Macduff rode for the most part in deep gloom. Then, ahead, showed the broad sunlit space of a clearing, jade green grama grass spread over it like a soft carpet. At the fringe of timber, Macduff dismounted and searched the forest around him. But the only men seemed to be the dead ones, lying there in the sun of the clearing, flies making a lazy, funereal buzz around their bodies. It must have been a big fight.

The man nearest Macduff was an Apache, and he remembered there had been the unshod prints of an Indian's pony among those he had been following. Farther on were two hard-faced young peons, both wearing Colts buckled around their dirty white cotton trousers. Sprawled across one of them was a man in more expensive clothes, silk-lined riding cloak hitched up over his head and hiding his face, blood spreading blackly over the back of his embroidered Spanish vest. And on across the meadow were two more, in the same cloak and vest.

The tracks Macduff had been following led right into the clearing. He stood there for ten minutes, searching the forest around the glade carefully, and it seemed silent, empty. Even so, the safer thing would have been to skirt the clearing and see if he couldn't pick up the trail on the other side. He was about to do that when he caught sight of another body, half hidden in the grass.

Cautiously Macduff stepped into the open, leading his gelding. He passed the Apache, and the richly dressed man sprawled over the two peons, and the pair of bodies beyond them. Then he stood looking down at that last one.

He was short and thick-set, dressed in Yankee jeans and a dark fustian, gold watch chain gleaming across his white waistcoat. His brown hair curled long down the back of his neck, and though the sun had burned his face to an Indian darkness, it hadn't quite obliterated the Irish freckles on his snub nose.

Armijo and the others had never seen the man they expected to bring the money, but they had been given his description. And now Macduff could well see why they had taken him for James Riley.

In Macduff's four years at Bent's, he had seen enough men die when they became careless. He knew, suddenly, how careless he had been. But now it was too late.

"I'm disappointed in you, *señor* . . . I always thought El Cojo would be a harder man to snare," said a voice behind Macduff. It was the same sardonic tone Danny had heard in the Costillo *hacienda* the night before.

Macduff turned, keeping his hand carefully away from his gun. The man who had spoken sat a big black just outside the fringe of timber behind Macduff. Over the man's grease-slick leggings were a pair of gaudy Apache boot moccasins of deerskin, long enough to reach the hip, folded over until they were knee-high, forming a double thickness of hide as protection against the clawing brush.

"Well," said Macduff, "Anton Chico. And what did you do with the girl?"

The *bandido* held a big Dragoon pistol in his right hand, single-action hammer at full cock under his thumb. He waved the gun at the richly dressed man sprawled across the bodies of the white-trousered peons.

"That is *Señor* Carlos Farrerra. And those other *cabrónes* in the cloaks are men of the Farrerra party. They said they'd give me half the money they got from Riley if I met them here this morning with the girl. As soon as I handed her over, they jumped me. I should have known a bunch of small-time *politicos* like them wouldn't part with any fifteen thousand silver dollars. They could have finished my tortillas right then. But the fools started shooting while I and some of my men were still on our horses."

"But why should they want the girl?" asked Macduff.

Anton Chico's sardonic mouth tightened impatiently. "The Costillo party plans to storm the *palacio* and take Armijo themselves if the money doesn't reach him by tonight. Naturally the Farrerras don't want that any more than they want Armijo to get the money. Either way he's out of the office, and they fall with him. When the Costillos find the Farrerras have the girl, their leader, they won't dare make a move, knowing it would mean her life."

There were four wild *ladrónes* behind Anton

Chico, sitting jaded horses just under the fringe of pine, their eyes filled with the fierce wildness of the lobo wolf that has run alone for so long he doesn't know what it is to feel safe. One of them had a ragged serape over his left shoulder and a big Green River knife through a broad belt of Cheyenne wampum. Down one side of his face, from temple to jawbone, the flesh had been laid open. He gave Macduff a murderous glance, and Macduff realized it must be the man he had pistol-whipped the night before.

"Let's not palaver here like a bunch of *duennas*, *jefe*," he said to Anton Chico. "The dragoons will be coming sooner or later. They must have heard our guns."

Anton Chico leaned forward in his silver-mounted California saddle, flapping his legs out wide for support. Only then did Macduff see how he held his left hand tightly over his side.

"*Sí, compadre*, you are right," he growled, then he nodded indifferently toward the dead Apache in the grass. "They got my Indian. I managed to escape with these four *hombres*. We waited up on the slope till the Farrerras left with the woman, then tried to follow their trail. But the Apache was my tracker, and we lost it down by Río Espíritu Santo. I remembered how you ran out of the house last night, and figured you would be following us. I came back here to wait for you. And now, El Cojo, you're going to follow the trail of those Farrerras, if necessary, all the way to hell."

"If you know I'm El Cojo, why did you take my mules last night?" asked Macduff bitterly.

"I thought you were Riley then. My Apache recognized you when you chased us into the street last night. . . ." Suddenly the sharp intelligence in Anton Chico's black eyes was turned into a vicious, impatient anger. "You ask too many questions, *señor*. I took a hunk of lead in that fight, and I've lost a lot of blood, and I want to catch those Farrerras before I fall off my *caballo* like a drunk . . . a *borrachón*. Now get on your horse and start tracking, or I'll shoot you in the legs and make you follow the trail on your hands and knees."

The tracks were easy to follow to the Río Espíritu Santo—Holy Ghost Creek. Macduff followed the hoof prints of some ten horses down into the water. They didn't come out on the other bank.

"They've either gone upstream or down," said Macduff. "Using the water to hide their tracks."

"Obviously," said Anton Chico. "And now, *señor*, you had better live up to the things the Apaches tell of you . . . if you understand me."

He waved his Dragoon, and Macduff saw what he meant. Either way he stood to lose. If he couldn't find the trail now, the *bandido* would kill him. And if he did find it, when they reached the end, Anton Chico would kill him anyway.

Yet he had to finish the thing now. The Farrerras had killed his brother; he owed them for that. Also, they held the lives of countless American troops in their hands, and they had the woman.

With infinite patience, he coursed up and down the stream, hunting for sign. He spent much time where the thickets of chokecherry and wild rose reached out over the water. Anton Chico had carried Lajara across the withers of his mount. If her head was still hanging over on one side, if the horse had passed near the bank. . . . Finally he found a strand of blue-black hair caught in a thorny bramble that stretched out over the cutbank. It was about a mile upstream from where the tracks had entered the water. He straightened, standing knee-deep in the icy stream, holding the hair up for Anton Chico to see.

The *bandido* sat on the bank, the four *ladrónes* nervous behind him. He grinned sardonically. "*Señor*, if the Apaches said you could trail a bald eagle, I wouldn't doubt them. It is unfortunate you were born an honest man. Your talent could be put to so many better uses than hunting for Bent's Fort."

Macduff mounted his gelding, slapped his wet legs against its flanks to stir his circulation. "And when we find the Farrerras, how do you know they'll have the money?"

The bandit spurred his black into the shallows

after Macduff, turning upstream. "You saw *Señor* Riley there in the clearing. The Farrerras wanted him stopped last night. All they had to do was let me know he was due at *Señorita* Costillo's *hacienda* with the money. Then, you came instead. When I found beaver pelts instead of silver, I got in touch with the Farrerras. They still thought you were Riley, thought you'd come ahead as a decoy, leaving someone else to bring the money. They headed back toward Las Vegas to intercept whoever that was, telling me they'd give me half the money anyway if I'd get the girl and bring her to that clearing. Riley must have been late, and they caught him somewhere in Apache Pass, because they'd already killed him when I arrived with the girl."

Macduff started as a long-legged *paisano* was flushed from some wild plum bushes on the bank. He hadn't realized how keyed up he was.

"What's the matter, El Cojo?" The *bandido* grinned. "Are you getting nervous?"

Macduff didn't answer, because he had caught sight of prints leaving the creek. The horses were glad to get out of the cold water. Blowing and snorting, they passed through the aspens fringing the stream, yellowing with summer color, then through the pines that covered the lower slopes, the thick blanket of needles muffling the hoof beats.

It was harder to follow the trail through those

needles, and Macduff had to dismount. They were rising steadily, and though it was growing colder, Macduff could feel the sweat moistening his palms. The growing excitement made him breathe hard, leaving his senses abnormally acute. He had faced many kinds of death before, but not this certain, waiting kind, his life hanging on the shortening time, and on the cocked hammer under Anton Chico's thumb.

They had left the carpet of needles behind and Macduff could read sign from the saddle again. He swung aboard the gelding, glad for that at least. He wanted to be mounted when it came. There was little enough chance that way.

"All right, *señor*, we have come far enough!" called Anton Chico softly.

Macduff could see it now, the black hole in the side of the cliff, partly hidden by brambles and scrub oak. A big bunch of jaded horses stood before the cave with a knot of men dressed in riding cloaks, high black boots and heavily glazed sombreros.

"Farrerras," muttered Anton Chico. "Small-time *politicos* that grew fat under Armijo's rule and stand to lose everything if he runs out on them."

Macduff wasn't looking at the cave any longer. He knew that if Anton Chico wanted to take the Farrerras by surprise, he wouldn't risk a shot down here. It would come from behind, then, from one of Chico's men, and the *bandido* was just talking to cover whatever they were going to do.

"I've heard of this cave in Cañon Espíritu Santo," said Chico. "Some say it leads to subterranean passages that open out in the mountains above the Nambe Pueblo."

Beneath Chico's voice, Macduff heard the swift swishing sound he'd been waiting for, the sound of a man's cotton-sleeved arm raising for a blow.

With a sudden jerk to the side, Macduff kicked his gelding's right flank, and yanked cruelly on the big Spanish bit. The horse danced hard into Chico's black. Throwing himself at the *bandido*, Macduff heard the man behind him grunt with having missed the blow, heard the slide of his leggings over leather as he tried to stop himself from going out of the saddle.

The Irishman was already crashing into Chico, putting all his chips on the bet that the *bandido* wouldn't use his gun. He felt the muzzle of that Dragoon dig into his belly, then both of them were slamming down off the black and onto the ground.

V

They hit hard. Macduff was on top with that gun still sinking into his belly. All the air went out of Anton Chico in a big burst. Macduff tried to grab the gun. Chico wrenched it from between their bodies, holding his thumb desperately across that cocked hammer, striking at Macduff.

Head rocking to the blow, Macduff sprawled flat on the man, clawing at the gun. Then the steel of a blade, burning like fire, slipped through his ribs from the back. The man he had pistol-whipped the night before straightened, the bloody knife in his hand, and Macduff collapsed across Anton Chico. The bandit heaved off Macduff and stood up, face twisted with pain, left hand going again to the wound in his side.

"I knew he wouldn't give up without a fight," he panted. "*Por Dios*, I didn't expect a lame man to move so fast!"

The first pain held Macduff in a strange lethargy. Dimly he could hear Chico's voice, the shuffle of feet. He knew he would be helpless against that second thrust. He wished, somehow, that he could have seen the girl again. It would have been easier to die. . . . He saw the blurred figure of the *ladrón* with the knife move to stab him again, then Anton Chico grabbed the man's arm, growling angrily: "*Caracoles*, you're wasting time. I can't last much longer with this bullet hole through me and you want to stand around putting that knife in a man you've already killed. Look at all the blood on him, you *cabrón*! He was dead before you pulled the blade out."

They moved away up the hill, and only the horses stood there, cropping half-heartedly at some bark. Tentatively Macduff raised to an elbow. Pain stabbed at him, subsided. The bandit leader and two of his men were working up through thinning timber toward the cave. The other two *ladrónes* had worked around above the Farrerras, were sliding down through the knee-high clumps of wild hops that grew on the slope over the cave mouth.

Macduff crawled on his hands and knees to Chico's black, the nearest horse. He reached up and grasped the stirrup, hauled himself to his knees, then to his feet. He leaned weakly against the horse, breathing the stink of sweaty leather.

Then the guns opened up. Anton Chico and two of his men broke from the edge of the timber, firing. And the pair above the cave rose up, six-shooters clattering. The Farrerras were taken completely by surprise. One of them folded without a sound. Another took a half step forward, clawing spasmodically at his gun, then fell over on his face. The other two whirled wildly toward the cave. One of them made it.

The two *ladrónes* above slid down the shale over the cave's mouth and dropped to the ground. Anton Chico and his pair joined them, and they all disappeared into the black maw.

Macduff let go of the black and staggered from the junipers toward the cave, every step a separate agony. Chico had taken his gun, and he stopped a moment beside one of the dead Farrerras, stooping for the man's weapon. Black nausea swept him and he felt himself falling. It was a terrific effort of will that jerked him erect, the dead man's six-shooter clutched in his fist. Then he swayed toward the cave, footsteps fumbling into the cool darkness, the smell of rich black loam softly enveloping him.

A blast of gunfire sounded from farther back, rolling down to Macduff in warped, hollow echoes. And then came Anton Chico's wild laughter. And silence again.

When the Irishman came across the first bodies, it was still quite light in the cave. The Farrerras must have made a stand here, because Anton Chico's four men were sprawled on the black earth, one after another, and beyond them a little huddle of Farrerras in their cloaks and boots and rich vests. Macduff had just moved past when a sudden movement on his right whirled him.

Two dim shapes hurtled from a recess in the caves. Macduff caught a flapping cloak, light glinting along a sword blade. He jerked backward, trying to dodge the sword, gun bucking up in his hand with the first shot.

One of the men went down. Macduff's thumb was snapping his hammer back for the second shot when the other man smashed up against him, carrying him back against the opposite wall of the cave.

With his gun against the man's body, Macduff fired. The sound of the explosion was muffled.

For a moment he thought he had missed, and with the sword quivering in him like that, he wondered why he felt no pain. Then the body against him relaxed, and slid down to the ground, limp hand falling from the rapier hilt, leaving the sword sticking there.

For a long moment, Macduff sagged against the wall, looking down at the man. The sightless eyes that stared up so gruesomely were those of *Don* Gaspar Jamarillo, the man who had put that same blade through Terrance, back at the *hacienda*. Macduff knew a moment of grim satisfaction— that score, at least, was settled. Then he saw why he felt no pain. He had managed to dodge the rapier, after all, and the blade had only gone through the sleeve of his buffalo coat, pinning him to the cave's wall. He pulled it free, dropped it, stepped across Jamarillo.

If the *don* had let Anton Chico go on by, then there might well be other Farrerras who had done the same thing, not wanting to meet the *bandido's* skill with the Dragoon pistol.

That last effort seemed to have taken all the will to move from Macduff. Fighting an enveloping lethargy, he stumbled into the darkening recesses of the tunnel, and the thought of the woman back there somewhere was the only thing that kept him going. Lajara . . .

There was another clatter of gunfire, and flame stabbed the gloom ahead of Macduff. Anton Chico's voice followed, calling to someone: "It's only you and me left now, isn't it? You've played your pretty game for a long time! Nobody would have guessed you were the real leader of the Farrerras. But you can't double-cross everybody all of the time, and you made a mistake when you tried it on me. This is Anton Chico, you fat *cabrón*, and I'm coming to kill you. I'm coming to get the money and kill you!"

The answering voice was so muffled and warped that Macduff couldn't recognize it: "Don't come around that turn, Chico, you won't stand a chance."

There was the sound of a moving body, pounding feet, a crazy yell. Then guns drowned everything else.

Macduff heard the *bandido* scream once in mortal pain. The echoes of the gunfire and of the scream slapped mournfully back and forth down the tunnel until they died.

There was a turn ahead, then, and the mysterious leader of the Farrerras was beyond it. Whoever tried to get him would be going from a lighter part of the cave to a darker part, and would be a perfect skylighted target—would die, as Anton Chico had died.

Forcing himself ahead, against that pain and lethargy, Macduff stumbled over another body. He went down, dropping his gun. The man he had tripped over was another Farrerra. His hand still clutched the ornate butt of a six-gun that had been so useless against Anton Chico's deadly Dragoon. Yet, not even Anton Chico's gun skill had been able to meet the unknown leader of the *ricos nuevos* around that turn.

Terrance had said that the unknown Ferrerra leader was the most dangerous of all. Danny could believe it now, because Terrance was dead, like Farrerra himself, and Anton Chico with all his *ladrónes* were dead. And, too, all the Ferrerra *ricos nuevos* . . . And now only that man beyond the turn remained, with everything his own way, playing the game out with all the top cards in his hand.

What could Macduff hope for? Nothing but what Chico had gotten, what all the others had gotten.

The Irishman must have made considerable noise in falling, for that muffled voice around the turn called out: "That you, Jamarillo?"

Macduff was concentrating too hard on finding his gun to pay much attention. He hardly heard. Then he found the weapon, the bone handle covered with cool black loam.

"Jamarillo?" came the voice again, still muffled and unrecognizable.

Macduff shook his head to clear it, tried to place the voice. It had a familiar ring, a tantalizing familiarity. Then the man chuckled.

"All right, so it isn't Jamarillo. Come on around the corner and you'll get the same thing Chico got. Macbeth had the right idea . . . 'I bear a charmed life, which must not yield to one of woman born.' "

Suddenly Macduff knew who was waiting there for him, knew who had led the Ferrerra party all along. His voice boomed down the cavern in hollow, ghostly answer.

"Don't you remember the rest of it, Doctor? 'Despair thy charm, and tell the angel thou hast served. Macduff was from his mother's womb untimely ripped.' "

There was a moment of stunned silence. Macduff took it to fight erect. He was so weak he had to lean against the wall for support. He couldn't seem to think straight, and finally, to focus his thoughts, he began saying a name. It gave him strength, somehow: *Lajara, Lajara . . .*

Dr. Leo Britt's chuckle came finally, and it sounded forced. "If it isn't our lame Irishman, by Harry! And I thought that Macduff business was just some of your blarney. Sorry I got you into this, really. You caused me no end of trouble. I didn't realize who you really were until my Farrerras picked up the real Riley in Apache Pass. But you won't cause any more trouble, will you, not if you try to come around that corner?"

The woman's voice was high with fear. "Macduff, don't do it. You'll make a perfect target. Chico couldn't do it. You won't stand a chance!"

Lajara's voice sent a new power coursing through him, and he jerked away from the support of the wall, wiping his sweaty hand against his leggings, then slipping the gun into it. He began moving forward in a half-blind stumble.

Yet he'd be a fool to march around and take it like Chico had. That was the normal way, though, to go around the turn standing up. Britt would expect him to come that way. It would take eyes a moment to accustom themselves to the darker portion of the tunnel. And that moment would be all Dr. Leo Britt's. He couldn't miss.

A black curtain kept sliding over Macduff's eyes. The cave reeled around him. He wanted to lie down and give way to the pain and cry like a baby.

"Macduff, don't be a fool . . . !"

It was Lajara's voice, and it was the spur. Teeth clamped shut, he gathered himself for that last rush. Then he began to run, his gun coming up, his square, broad-shouldered body moving into a pounding, lop-sided charge, moving so much faster than anyone would expect of a lame man. And in his mind was that single driving thought: *Lajara . . .*

On the last step that took him banging around the curve, he launched himself into a low dive, body hurtling forward from the vertical to the horizontal just an instant before Dr. Britt's gun flamed from the gloom.

The lead whined over Macduff and plopped into earth behind him.

It wasn't as dark as Macduff had thought, and in that instant before he hit on his belly, his eyes became accustomed to the gloom, and he could see the doctor back against the cave's wall. Spasmodic anger at having missed that first time twisted the doctor's pudgy face, and his thumb was twitching the hammer back for a second shot, gun jerking down toward Macduff's hurtling body.

Then the Irishman moved, sliding along on his belly, rocks ripping his coat and flannel shirt from collar to belt, head rocking as his chin slammed into the ground. But somehow he had managed to keep his gun out in front, holding it desperately in both hands. And even as he began to slide forward, he shot.

Britt stood there for one moment, face blank

with surprise and pain—as if he really believed he bore a charmed life and couldn't understand how Macduff had hit him. Then he took a faltering step backward, trying stubbornly to catch at his gun's hammer again.

It took all Macduff had left to lift his six-shooter and fire again. The doctor dropped his gun and went over backward.

For a long time Macduff tried to gather the strength to crawl to the woman, where she lay beside Riley's Mexican pack saddles, bulging with the silver. He managed to get his Green River out, finally, and cut her loose from the rawhide lashings. She helped him up, then was suddenly in his arms, sobbing with reaction.

"It was the doctor all along," she cried. "With the backing of the Farrerra party, he was going to overthrow Armijo after the governor had ambushed the *Americanos* . . . was going to take over the government himself. He was the master conspirator of all, and none of us suspected. Not even Armijo."

Her voice had drowned whatever sound Valdez must have made coming in.

"What have you been doing, *señor?*" he asked. "It looks like the Taos Massacre."

Macduff tried to keep himself from falling with the girl's weight against him. "I thought you were in Santa Fe, Captain."

"When the money didn't come, Armijo sent

me out with final orders for the preparation of the ambush," said Valdez. "A few hours ago, we heard the first firing. I thought the *Americanos* had flanked us, and took five squadrons up the slope. We finally found that clearing. And then we heard more firing from up Cañon Espíritu Santo."

"There's your money," said Macduff, motioning to the *aparejos*. "You're about the only man I'd trust it with. You can take your five squadrons and get it back to Armijo today."

"*Sí*," said Valdez. "Just in time, too. We have already received word that Kearny has taken Las Vegas and is advancing on Santa Fe. . . ."

He stopped talking, because the girl had taken one of her arms from around Macduff and was staring at the blood on her hand, eyes widening.

"It's all right," said Macduff, weakly. "I was jerking around a lot when they stabbed me. Makes me sort of dizzy . . . just lost a lot of blood."

She put her arm around him, supporting his weight. "I don't think the blade is made that could kill you, not after coming all the way from Santa Fe with every *hombre* in the city looking for you, getting through all the peons and Armijo's dragoons and Anton Chico and his *bandidos*, and the Farrerras, and the doctor. I didn't believe any man could be that good. But I do now. . . ."

He found it hard to choose the right words,

because his head was swimming, and because he always felt awkward with a woman, anyway. "Some men come West to run away from something, others hunting something. I guess I was hunting something. Only last night, when Anton Chico took you, did I realize what it was . . . what every man hunts for, whether he knows it or not. . . ."

She seemed to understand, for her arms were soft around him and her eyes were shining. "You'll like it in Santa Fe now that everything is settled, Danny Macduff," she said softly.

And he knew she spoke the truth.

Satan's Keyhole

I

It was one of Downieville's quiet nights. In front of the St. Charles House, Sydney Duck was getting forty lashes for pilfering sluice boxes on Goodyear's Bar. In Rogue Alley, Poker Nye was standing the whole town to drinks with the $30,000 in gold dust he had panned out of Musketo Creek in one week. In Main Street, a crowd of shouting miners carried *Signora* Biscaccianti and her grand piano on their shoulders to the hall where she was to give her concert.

In the Washington Bar, Glenn Anders was getting drunk. He sat alone at one of the short card tables in a corner of the smoky, crowded room. He was walled off from it all, shut up in a world of his own, a world of one single bitter thought. He hadn't found her. It was the only thing he could think of. He had spent two years and every cent he owned hunting for her, and, when he had been so close he could almost smell her perfume, he had failed. Tomorrow he would have to go to pick and panning along Goodyear's Bar to stay alive. By the time he had any stake she would be as far out of his reach as she had been in the beginning.

He cursed and took another long drink from the

bottle. The cheap Chinese gin blinded him and he set the bottle down and squinted his eyes till they stopped watering. In these California mining camps it was cheaper for a man to drink himself to death than to sustain life with food or shelter. A slice of bread was $1, and a filthy pallet with twenty other men in a room at the St. Charles was $2, but if Hangtown Charlie had been through town recently, a man could get a bottle of his infamous gin in Rogue Alley for 50¢. And it had been Glenn Anders's last four bits.

He placed his elbows on the table and put his head in his hands. It was a big head for a big man and all his yellow hair made it look even bigger, the way a lion looks bigger because of its mane. It lay in a tangled mat all the way down the back of his neck, almost black with grease and dirt except for the silver streaks where the sun had bleached it. His beard was three weeks old and two inches long and the color of pay dirt.

Anders heard a chair scrape and looked up to see a man seating himself across the table. He was a little man, narrow, shriveled and drawn, as if some sickness or some inner smallness were pinching him in. He had a sharp, foxy face and the traditional notch of the Sydney Duck in his ear—those freed or escaped convicts who had flooded California from the British penal colonies in Australia.

"Dusty's the name, guv'ner," he said.

"You picked the wrong table," Anders said. "I can't buy you a drink."

"Maybe I can buy you one, guv'ner. Or tell you where your wife is."

Anders sat up so violently that he knocked the bottle over.

Dusty grinned. Then he said: "Hangtown Charlie told me your story, Anders. He said that his last run through here you got drunk on his gin and spilled the whole thing."

Anders leaned across the table and grabbed the man's dirty Mackinaw in both hands. "If you know . . . where is she, damn you, where is she?"

Dusty made no attempt to pull Anders's hands loose. "Grass Valley, Anders. We had a stopover there while we waited for the northbound stage. She was givin' a performance at the theater. On the playbill they called her Jamaica."

Anders held the man against the table, staring at him. There was a pressure behind Anders's eyes. It was hard to breathe. He wanted to believe. He couldn't believe. Slowly his hands slid off the Duck's coat, dropped to the table. Dusty must have seen the defeat in his eyes.

"Maybe you ain't got the fare to Grass Valley," he said.

"You knew that already," Anders said bitterly.

The Duck smiled slyly. He wiped his mouth with the back of a freckled hand. "Well, guv'ner, if you was to try and walk to Grass Valley, she'd

75

be gone before you got halfway there, wouldn't she? But what if you had the fare?"

"What do you want?" Anders said. "What do you get out of this?"

Dusty grinned. "Whyn't you come with me and see?"

Drunk though he was, suspicious though he was, Anders could not quell the excitement in him. All he could think of was Jamaica. Dusty stood up, waiting. Anders studied the raddled face a moment longer, then rose. Together they pushed their way out of the crowded Washington Bar into the freezing winter night. Anders shivered violently and fumbled to button his tattered Mackinaw, stumbling down Main toward the river. It was too dark to see the towering mountains that surrounded the deep basin in which the handful of shacks was huddled. It was February, 1854, and the Yuba's North Fork was still full of ice beneath the rickety bridge that led to Jersey Flat. On the Jersey side Anders passed the long black mass of Cut-Eye Foster's store and saw the dim lights of the stage station ahead.

In front of the Wells, Fargo office pitch-pine flares cast a garish light over a mule train from Marysville that was being unloaded. A hundred exhausted jacks brayed and bucked and kicked up dirty snow while the cursing packers fought frozen hitches with numb fingers. Anders had to pick his way through the mêlée to gain the station.

He passed a bearded giant, ripping a tarp off the heap of goods on his pack. The jackass cat-backed just as the man pulled out a diamond hitch. Anders dodged aside to keep from being inundated by a rain of canned tomatoes. Another animal wheeled broadside. Flour barrels were balanced precariously in the slings on either side of the crosstree and one slammed into Anders, almost knocking him off his feet.

He reached the battered Concord, standing squarely before the door, a mud wagon with the pine flares making a yellow gleam on its scarred birch paneling. The tongue was dropped and it had no team in harness. The conductor was lifting some luggage out of the boot. Anders saw that it was Hangtown Charlie, the Chinese conductor who made the run biweekly from Hangtown. Pigtailed, topped with a conical bamboo hat, his head looked like an incongruous bronze moon perched on the shaggy brown mass of his buffalo coat. He giggled when he saw Anders.

"Solly, Mistuh Anduhs. Cholly he no got any gin this tlip."

Before Anders could answer, a woman moved from the black shadow of the wooden overhang. Anders saw that she was very young, not much more than a girl. Her face seemed buried in the upturned collar of her fur coat. Beneath a saucy beaver hat he could see a few honey-yellow curls, and wide blue eyes. The chill had put strawberry marks in her cheeks.

"Mister Anders," she said, "I'm Opal Mason."

He frowned at her. She was a perfect stranger to him. He asked: "Any kin to Colonel Mason?"

"I'm his niece. My father is Garrett Mason, the colonel's brother. Dad and I were in San Francisco when you were building the Illinois Central with the colonel. The colonel talked about you in his letters."

Anders remembered that Colonel Mason had mentioned a brother who was a mining engineer. "Well, Miss Mason, I'm glad to meet you, but right now . . ."

"Give me a minute, Mister Anders. I've come all the way from Hangtown to find you." She hesitated, then motioned toward a shadowy figure behind her. "Missus Riley came with me."

Mrs. Riley moved out. She was a fat woman in a ratty fur coat. China-blue eyes were almost buried in her doughy Irish face. She looked Anders up and down. *"Humph,"* she said.

Quickly Opal said: "You've heard of the Mason Water Company?"

Anders had heard snatches of talk in the Downieville saloons. "The company formed to bring water to the mines?"

"That's it," she said. "This hydraulic mining has developed a demand for water the local sources can't begin to fill. So the miners at Hangtown formed the water company and got my father to engineer the job. They'll bring the water from the Rubicon, up near its source. Dad had almost fifty miles of flume and ditch built when he reached Satan's Keyhole. . . ."

"The what?"

"A gorge north of Hangtown. You've never seen such a gash. Dad tried three times to bridge it. Each time the bridge went down. The third time . . . the third time he went with it."

"I'm sorry."

"It didn't kill him. But he won't be out of bed for some time. The bridge has to go up before spring thaw, Mister Anders, or the project will fail."

Anders looked at Dusty. He began to understand why the little Duck had brought him here.

Anders said: "Your father's in the business, Miss Mason. He must know . . . he can't be that desperate. . . ."

"Of course he knows, Mister Anders. You had some bad luck. . . ."

"Bad luck?" His voice was bitter.

After a moment's silence she said: "We're making you an offer. It's legitimate and there aren't any strings. Dad thinks you're the only man in California who can get that bridge across Satan's Keyhole. When he heard you were in Downieville . . ."

"Heard?"

"Hangtown Charlie told us, the last time he came in from here. He said you were . . . you got . . ."

"Drunk," Anders supplied. He passed a hand over his eyes. Drunk as a sailor, and spilling his guts to a Chinese conductor—he hardly remembered it. How much had he told that smiling Chinese?

"Well," Opal said, "we couldn't pay you all in cash, but there would be shares in the company, and once the water was delivered the shares would skyrocket. . . ."

He shook his head. "I can't do it. Charlie apparently told you about my wife. I'm out here hunting her. Dusty said you saw her. . . ."

Mrs. Riley stirred belligerently. "If y'r wife's named Jamaica, and she's with the King's Players, we saw her at Grass Valley. *The Bohemian Girl*. If Missus Knight created that part o' the Gypsy Queen, y'r wife demolished it. Voice like a banshee, makin' faces all the time, wavin' her arms like a signalman. . . ."

He closed his eyes, wincing. The description was devastatingly accurate. Yet it was only one side of Jamaica, only one of the pictures he had remembered from these last two years. It wasn't the image he had held in his mind when he arrived in San Francisco less than a month ago, closer to Jamaica than at any other time during his long search. Only a week behind the King's

Players, he had followed their trail upriver to Sacramento, on through Marysville, and Rough and Ready. Arriving at Downieville, he had found that he was three days too late. They must have taken a private democrat wagon out of town. California Stage hadn't got their fares and nobody knew their destination. And he had less than $3 in his pocket. That night Hangtown Charlie was in Downieville on his biweekly run. He had personally sold Anders the first bottle of gin. Anders had bought the succeeding bottles from one of Charlie's Chinese salesmen in Rogue Alley. . . .

"Do you have the fare to Grass Valley?" Opal Mason asked. Anders didn't answer. He didn't have to. She was looking at his stubble beard, his worn clothes. She said: "If I pay your way to Grass Valley, and you see your wife, will you come on to Hangtown afterward and take a look at the bridge?"

"I couldn't make a promise like that."

"Mister Anders, these theatrical companies tour the mines every year. If the King's Players are making their regular circuit, they'll be heading toward Hangtown anyway."

He felt trapped, suffocated by a sense of panic. He couldn't let Jamaica get away again—couldn't lose this last chance.

"I won't ask you to commit yourself any further than that," Opal said. "Just talk to my father

and see the bridge . . . and your fare is paid."
He looked at her a long time. Then his head
bowed and he moved past her to the door. As he
pulled it open, the light fell on a tattered placard
nailed to the wall.

CALIFORNIA STAGE CO.
Office, Orleans Hotel
Second Street, Between J and K, Sacramento
J. BIRCH—PRESIDENT
DAILY CONCORD COACHES

Leave the Orleans Hotel, carrying the U. S.
Mail via: Marysville and Shasta. Touching
at Charley's Rancho, Bidwell's Rancho,
Hamilton City, Oak Grove, Clear Creek,
Lawson's, Tehama, Campbell's Rancho,
Red Bluffs, Cotton Wood Creek, One
Horse Town, Middletown, Covertsburg,
Shasta, Yreka and Pitt River Diggings . . .

There was more, but he couldn't find Grass
Valley so he went on in. A white-headed station-
master was asleep in a chair before a stove
with cast-iron columns that were fluted and
pedimented like a Greek temple. His boots lay
beside him and his feet, with three pairs of socks
on, were toasting on the rail in front of the stove.
He had taken the fancy ornament off the boiling
hole to put on a tea kettle. Its screaming whistle

made Anders grit his teeth. He crossed and moved the kettle off. The whistle died to a low moan. Anders shook the stationmaster. The old man started up.

"Southbound at ten o'clock," he chanted. "Thirty pounds per passenger, any baggage over that four-bits a pound, Mountain House, Camptonville, Grass Valley. . . ."

"All right, pop," Anders said. "That's what I wanted to know."

The old man settled back, not yet fully awake. "Shouldn't come on a man so sudden. Liable to throw down on you."

Anders borrowed a razor and some of the hot water. The stationmaster gave him a lighted candle. He carried it to the washroom at the rear, a tiny cubicle containing a tarnished mirror, a soiled roller towel, and a cake of lye soap strong enough to strip the hide off an elephant. After shaving, he stepped outside looking for the water butt that usually stood behind these stations. He dunked his head. The icy shock ran through his whole body. He straightened, gasping and blowing. He felt a pressure against his back like the end of a pole digging into his ribs.

From behind him a man said: "I thought you'd be wanting to sober up sooner or later."

Anders didn't move. The icy water dripped off his soaked mane and ran beneath his shirt. He looked over his shoulder. A row of bottles glassed in the narrow back window of the stage station. A faint glow came through them and touched the man behind Anders, a man turned immense by a matted grizzly-bear coat that stank like rancid bacon. He wore a battered black bowler hat and a pair of curling side whiskers that were turning silver at the edges. His face had a curiously etched look. Countless tiny lines grained the cheeks. Each line was a dark thread in the flesh, as though dirt had been ground into it for a lifetime and could never quite be washed away. He was holding a gun in Anders's back.

"Well, Cousin Jack," Anders said.

The gun dug deeper into his back. The man said sharply: "Where'd you hear my name?"

"I thought it's what they called all you Cornishmen around the camps," Anders said.

Cousin Jack didn't answer immediately. The scent of his bearskin coat crept against Anders, pungent, animal. Finally the man said: "You ain't going to Hangtown."

"I'm going to Grass Valley."

"You ain't going anywhere. You ain't even getting on that coach."

Cousin Jack jammed the gun harder into his back, pushing Anders away from the building. The man kept the gun against him all the way, driving him through a clutter of dark shacks. Anders wondered if this was part of the pattern—

Dusty, the girl—but he couldn't make the connection. Too much happened, too fast.

They stumbled down the steep riverbank and picked their way through icy boulders till they were beneath the bridge. Cousin Jack took the gun out of Anders's back.

Anders ducked his head and threw up his left arm. It saved him. The gun struck his arm instead of his head. It was a vicious blow, numbing his arm and driving him to one knee.

He pivoted on his knee. He was dimly aware of Cousin Jack's immense shape above him, arm upraised to strike again. Anders caught the man's bearskin with his right hand and fell backward.

Cousin Jack was lunging forward to strike, completely off balance, and could not stop himself from going with Anders. As he rolled onto his back, Anders kept his grip on the bearskin, jackknifed his legs, and planted both feet in the big man's belly. Cousin Jack's own momentum flipped him completely over Anders. He landed on his back with a jarring thump.

Anders lurched to his feet, tearing open his Mackinaw to get at the Walker Colt holstered beneath. He heard Cousin Jack make a scrambling sound on his flank. He was barely able to see the man's bulk in the blackness beneath the bridge. He whipped his gun at what he thought was the man's head.

The blow almost tore the Walker from his

hand. Cousin Jack groaned sharply and his shape seemed to melt into the earth. Anders stood above him, panting heavily and waiting to strike again. Cousin Jack did not move.

Anders kneeled by the inert body. He fumbled with the bearskin until he got his hand beneath it, against the man's chest. A steady throb there told him Jack was still alive.

He tried to move the man but he was too heavy. Anders's left arm was numb and he felt sick; he could not wait for the Cornishman to recover. He was afraid of missing the coach. One thought was still uppermost in his mind. It didn't seem to matter what happened, all he could think about was Jamaica, and he didn't think he could stand it to miss her again. There had been too many defeats, too many frustrations, too many blind alleys.

He left the Cornishman and stumbled back to the station. He was drenched with sweat, despite the chill. At the back door he had to stop and lean against the building, so dizzy he thought he would fall. When it was over, he stepped inside.

Opal Mason and Mrs. Riley sat on a bench by the stove. Dusty stood in one corner. Opal rose from the bench when she saw Anders. He said: "A big Cornishman in a grizzly-bear coat . . . black bowler and side whiskers a mile long. . . ."

"Cousin Jack," she said.

"You know him?"

"What happened?" she asked.

"He tried to stop me . . . didn't want me going to Hangtown."

She took one hand from her muff. "It couldn't be, it simply couldn't be. . . ."

"Who is he, Miss Mason?"

"Why, Cousin Jack has been with us ever since I was a little girl. I don't understand. You must be mistaken. . . ."

"He's probably still under the bridge, if you want a look."

She turned helplessly to the Sydney Duck. Without a word the little man went out the back way. Opal started to follow.

"You stay here," Mrs. Riley said. "If he's there, Dusty can take care of him."

Opal stopped, looking again at Anders. He crossed the room and sat down. The old station-master had been watching it all, head cocked like a listening hound.

After a while Dusty came back in, shivering and grimacing. "Nobody's under the bridge," he said.

Opal looked at Anders and he said thinly: "I'm perfectly sober, Miss Mason. You have no explanation for this?"

"No," she said. "It doesn't make sense. Cousin Jack would have no reason, he would simply have no reason to . . . to . . ."

"To what?"

"That's it. What was he doing, Mister Anders?"

Anders shook his head. He couldn't think. The numbness was leaving his arm and it hurt too much even to try to think. He watched Opal Mason as she sat down again. She removed her porkpie hat. She had beautiful thick hair, the dull gleaming gold of the dust he had seen emptied from so many pokes onto the scales at Cut-Eye Foster's. She had not yet learned to pluck her brows; they were thick and heavy, twin golden sickles above the startlingly large blue eyes. There was something passionate and at the same time virginal about the pouting, little-girl shape of her lips. She was very young and she was very beautiful. She was the kind of girl he should have married.

So long ago . . . He leaned his head against the wall and closed his eyes and let those first years close in on him with a suffocating rush: 1849—shortly after he had returned from his studies in Europe—a junior engineer in one of the firms attending the preliminary meetings at New Orleans that were to culminate in the Southwestern Railroad Convention. He had first known Jamaica only by reputation. In a city of vivid and exotic personalities she shone with a luster all her own and her story could be heard from almost any young man in almost any café. Jamaica. He had thought it an affectation, at first, taking the name of the island of her birth. She had been born to the Creole aristocracy, the spoiled and pampered daughter of one of the richest French planters on Jamaica. The weevil and the slump of 1837 had wiped her father out. He had come to New Orleans with his family in a futile attempt to recoup his losses as a commission merchant. Jamaica's beauty had caught the elder Booth's eye, as he was touring the south, and his patronage had given her entrée to the theater world. When Anders arrived in New Orleans, she was the reigning star of the St. Charles.

There was an American company in town and the first time he saw her they were doing *Hamlet*. He was not an avid theatergoer but he had seen enough Shakespeare in London to know what an atrocious Ophelia she was doing. She mugged, grimaced, assumed outrageous poses, her dialogue was a stilted burlesque of Booth's consummate creations—and the audience loved it.

Anders couldn't help falling under the same spell. She was not an actress; she was a personality. She could have sat in a chair on the stage without saying a word and the house would have been filled every night. There was something electric about her, something more than her physical beauty.

The same thing happened to him when he met her at one of the after-theater soirées a few nights later. She seemed too vivid, too dramatic, too affected. Yet in a few moments he was fawning as avidly as the rest of the court fools who never left her side. It was the same spell she cast at the theater, ten times as devastating at close range. He had to compete with almost every other blade under fifty in the city. But he was already beginning to garner a reputation of his own. The alarming drop in river trade had hit New Orleans hard. The financial interests saw in the projected railroad an answer to all their prayers. Any man connected with it was looked upon as a local savior. Anders was, it was said, "that brilliant young engineer from Europe who's a-building the railroad to Nashville."

But when Jamaica got a bid to appear at Walleck's in New York, he had broken his contract to follow her. Their romance in New York had been a tempestuous affair, the talk of the theater world. He squandered most of his inheritance on her. One night they got drunk on champagne at a theater party, and woke up the next morning, married. . . .

"*Whoa,* you broncos, git back over that trace! Daisy, git, git!"

The raucous shout from outside the stage station jarred Anders. He looked around and the room came at him through the fading haze of memory. Dusty was warming himself by the stove and Mrs. Riley was nodding on the bench beside Opal.

"They're getting your stage ready," the station-master said.

Anders moved outside. Two Mexican hostlers were backing a six-hitch team into their traces. A wheeler had got his hind leg over the nigh trace and refused to step out of it. The horse was kicking spitefully at one of the famous ash wheels that no rain could swell and no heat could shrink. The driver stood under the overhang, stamping booted feet to restore circulation. He pointed a ferruled whip at the Mexicans and bawled: "Cut that damn' wheeler out and put Baldy in his place! I told you pack rats I wouldn't let another three-minute horse ruin my schedule."

Hangtown Charlie appeared from behind the coach, bowing ceremoniously as Opal appeared, and opened the door to help her in. Mrs. Riley was next. Thorough braces creaked and the mud wagon tilted as she put her ample weight on the step. It took both Anders and the Chinese to hoist her in. Anders followed, taking the front seat and facing Opal. Dusty was last. As he sat down, Anders saw the end of a slung-shot sticking from his coat pocket. It was the traditional weapon of the Ducks, a chunk of lead wrapped in leather and hung on a thong.

The door was slammed shut and Hangtown Charlie's face bobbed into the window like a Chinese jack-o'-lantern. "A jou'ney of a thousan' mile is taken step by step, an' the tlip to Hangtown bump by bump. Lao Tse once say that quiescence is mastuh of motion. Sit still an' you lide on glass."

He giggled and disappeared. The coach pitched as he climbed aboard and settled himself by the driver. Dusty saw Anders looking out at the stage yard and said: "You must 'ave been seein' snakes, mate. Cousin Jack couldn't o' been 'ere."

Anders looked at the sallow face. "What do you know about this?"

"Nothin', mate. A lot of nothin'."

II

The driver's bawling shout sent the broncos slamming into their collars. They roared out of Downieville. The coach rocked in its thorough braces like a skiff in a long swell and the wind rattled rolled leather curtains in the windows. They passed Goodyear's Bar, where Goodyear's Creek joined the Yuba, and the lights of the camp winked at them from the darkness. The coach jerked violently and Anders knew the broncos had hit their bearskin collars in their first upward surge against the steep Mountain House Grade. Anders was aware of the dim oval of Opal Mason's face in the darkness of the coach. He closed his eyes and it became Jamaica's face, turned ugly with the fury of their first battle.

It had been over money, a few weeks after they married. He had tried to budget what was left of his inheritance until he could make some contacts in New York. But Jamaica had no conception of what it meant to save. Her own salary did not begin to cover her extravagances, and he was still too infatuated to refuse her the slightest request. A month after the wedding they were dead broke.

When their credit was cut off, she blamed him. She left the hotel after the quarrel, and it took him a week to find her at the Union Place. There was an emotional reunion and Jamaica swore to be more sensible about money. The Erie was building the Mast Hope bridge that year and needed an assistant engineer. It was still a jerkwater railroad and Anders had enough recommendations and reputation to get the job despite the broken contract in New Orleans.

$800 a year was big money for an assistant. Jamaica was in another play at Walleck's and their life once more took on a frantic whirl. Ten hours a day on the location surveys or sweating over the profile maps in the office, rush home to change, dine at the Panorama, attend Jamaica's latest performance. After the show there was invariably a theater party, the glittering salons of the Odeon, the dim card rooms at Pinteaux's, the smoky pistol galleries at the Abbey, all merging finally into the struggle to keep awake through the drugged nightmare of Jamaica's lavish weekend parties, fighting for the three or four hours' sleep that would let him get back to the job in some semblance of wakefulness.

Somehow he got through to the finish. But rust hadn't even begun to form on the Mast Hope when it went down beneath a train. The engineer leaped to safety but a brakeman and two trainmen plunged to their death with the falling freight cars. If it had been a passenger train, the death toll would have gone into the hundreds. The investigation uncovered a series of flaws in the stressing that were traced to Anders.

It couldn't actually be said that they lived on Jamaica's salary, after that. They were too deep in debt. But as long as she was at Walleck's, she could still get enough credit on her name to keep up the pretense of high living. It was a bitter year for Anders. The Mast Hope catastrophe had branded him, and he could make connections nowhere.

Then Colonel Roswell Mason of Erie Canal fame was given a contract to build the Illinois Central. He interviewed Anders in his New Haven offices. The colonel was impressed, despite Mast Hope, and gave Anders a place on his corps of engineers. Jamaica was in the middle of a run and only after a dozen stormy battles did she agree to leave the play and go with him to Chicago.

She hated the town. She called it a pigsty on

a salt flat. It didn't help that she got a contract with Rice at the Chicago Theater. In a sort of rebellion she plunged even more deeply into the hectic theater life they had led in New York. Anders tried to keep up, but he felt her whirling farther and farther away from him. They were both at the breaking point. It came on the night a French count threw a diamond brooch across the footlights at her and she received a fantastic bouquet of flowers and wouldn't show Anders the card. They were shouting at each other when the count appeared at the dressing room door. Anders knocked the Frenchman down and Jamaica stormed out of the theater.

She wasn't at the hotel. Anders went on a binge. When he came out of it, he found he had lost a wife and a job. It was the beginning of his long search. New York, Savannah, New Orleans, Mexico City, following her trail from one glittering metropolis to the next, working at anything to support himself, to get another stake that would let him go on, wondering how any woman could make such a fool of a man.

The coach bucked and tilted, almost pitching Anders out of his seat. He caught himself, staring blankly at Opal Mason. He could hear the wild braying of mules outside and somebody shouting. Hangtown Charlie's bland face appeared at the window.

"Is said that wood cannot be watuh, and watuh cannot be stone. . . ."

"Dammit, mate," Dusty said, "don't give us any of your bright sayings. What's going on?"

"Fate assume many stlange shapes," Charlie said.

Anders made a disgusted sound and climbed out. Many of these roads had been built by private corporations that hadn't spent any more money than necessary. With the enormous cost of blasting shelf out of sheer granite cliffs there were places not wide enough for the passage of two vehicles. It was on one of these narrow ledges that the coach had come to a stop. Ahead was a freight outfit, two big Espinshied wagons with Sacramento Shippers signs on their sides. The lead span of their sixteen-hitch mule team was halted nose to nose against the two broncos at the head of the stage hitch.

The freighter stood near the lead mules, dimly visible in the moonlight. He was a kettle-bellied behemoth in greasy linsey-woolseys that were split at the seams by the immense girth of his thighs, and a blue wool shirt with most of the buttons popped off by the uncontainable barrel of his belly. His sleeves were rolled back from hairy forearms as big as Anders's legs. He seemed oblivious to the bitter cold. The stage driver was still on his perch, controlling the dancing broncos with one hand and beating his whip against his fancy foxed pants to emphasize each word.

"Kettle Corey, I ain't backing down to Goodyear's Bar for any Hangtown rum-pot and his sixteen brothers."

"Brothers, it is?" bawled the muleskinner. "Well, I'd rather eat at the same table with these mules than have the blood of those misbegotten sop-and-taters, five-minute glue-factory rejects in my veins. Is that bay mare your mother? The face bears resemblance. And maybe you can tell me how to back sixteen jacks and two ton of wagon and trailer a half-mile up the road to the Mountain House."

"Can't we settle it without all this?" Anders said to the driver. "The 'skinner has a point. What's to prevent you from backing down?"

"Only a mile of the narrowest road in the world before we hit a passing place," the driver said caustically. "The last man to try it with broncos like this went off at the first switchback. He must have got a good prayer in before he hit bottom."

Anders glanced over the cliff into the black maw of darkness. Opal climbed out, looking helplessly at the muleskinner.

"The driver called you Kettle Corey," she said.

The man grinned broadly. "That's me, ma'am."

"Isn't there anything we can do?" she asked.

The muleskinner softened. "If it war a democrat wagon, I'd say lower it over the side with ropes while I pass. The Concord's a mite heavy for that." Corey took an ivory snuffbox from his pocket, rolled some snuff into a ball, and tucked it under his lip. He scratched thoughtfully at his hairy chest. "I come up against a stage this way last year. They dismantled the thing and carried it around me piece by piece."

Anders looked at Charlie. "Is he joking?"

"No joke. Happen alla time. Abbot-Downing velly simple coach."

Anders squatted and looked at the thorough braces. They were manifold leather straps of the heaviest steer-hide. The body was suspended upon them and they acted both as springs for the coach and shock absorbers for the team.

"Mister," the stage driver said, "if you touch my coach, you'll never get a ride on California again."

Anders crawled under the coach and began to unshackle the braces. He heard the driver cursing him. Finally Hangtown Charlie crawled under to help him. The driver climbed down from his perch before they set the body on its brake beam. He stood to one side and he never stopped cursing. As they were detaching the front wheel carriage, Charlie got his finger pinched in a shackle. He let out a squeal and reared up, cracking his head.

"Consign Mister Abbott and Mister Downing to the fires of eternal hell," he said. He held his head and shook his pinched hand and squealed. "Condemn their eyes to be picked by crows and their entrails to be devoured by pigs and their bones ground to a dust so fine that no wind can carry a grain of it back to the Flowery Kingdom."

Anders looked at him in surprise. Charlie blinked and giggled.

"Excuse please. Captain of boat had fine pallot. Tell Chollie much fine cussing."

"It must have been quite a literate parrot," Anders said.

They left the detached front wheel carriage and tongue hitched to the broncos. They took the rear wheels off the axle and unloaded the luggage from the boot and the rack on top. The body accounted for more than a third of the over-all tonnage. The freighter pulled his team as close to the wall as possible while the three men rolled and upended and slid the wooden coach body past the mules and the towering Espinshied freight wagons. At the mile-high altitude it was a labor that exhausted the men. Anders was dripping sweat and completely spent when he returned for the team. His lungs burned and he ached all over.

He unhitched the off-leader and began taking it past the mules. The horse was excited by the strange activity and the smell of mules. It kept shying away from the edge of the cliff, rearing against the bit, ramming into the mules. Froth covered its snout and the eyes were rolling wildly. Anders realized then what an impossible job it would be to back six such animals down a mile of this road.

He was just beyond the muleskinner, who stood with his back against the head of the off-swing mule, when the mule jumped as though it had been burned. It let out a deafening bray and began to buck and thrash around in the harness. One of its lashing hind feet caught the horse in the ribs. The horse squealed, staggering against Anders and almost pushing him off the cliff. The frantic swinger had excited the other mules and the whole line was bucking and pitching.

Fighting with the bronco, Anders shouted: "Pull that jackass down by the ears, get him back against the wall!"

"I can't do nothing!" Kettle Corey shouted. "Get that crazy bronc' on past!"

"I can't! Your wheelers will kick me off! Get 'em quiet, damn you!"

Another kick struck the horse. It threw the bronco off balance and again it staggered into Anders. His boots slid on shale and he had the sense of the awesome drop at his back. The horse reared up, fighting to tear free. Anders knew he would go off if another kick pushed the animal against him. As he was fighting to pull the horse down and jerk it farther in on the road, he heard a mule's shoe thump against the bronco. All he could do was drop to his knees before the horse crashed into him. The staggering animal went over his body and off into empty air.

He clung to the rock shoulder at the very edge of the road, deafened by the bedlam from the mules. He crawled forward, sweating and trembling, and looked up. He saw that the excitement had infected the stage team. They were rearing and plunging while the driver and Charlie fought to hold them. Kettle Corey was lashing at his frantic mules with his twenty-foot whip. Its popper soared over the heads of the leaders and cracked in the face of the stage team's off-swinger. The horse went crazy.

He screamed and his wild rearing tore the bit out of Charlie's hand. The horse plunged blindly toward the edge of the road, pulling the others along. The driver shouted wildly and threw himself out of their way. The swinger went off first, his hind feet churning. The struggling wheelers snapped the tongue between them, just behind the double tree. It left the front wheels on the road when they went off. The last thing Anders saw was the broken tongue, still attached to the horses by tree and traces, flailing the empty air.

The mules were still milling and pitching. Anders fought his way down to their head, dodging their cow-kicks and their wildly swinging heads. When he was in the clear, he stopped. He saw Opal and Mrs. Riley and the three men from the stage still looking off into the chasm. He leaned against the rock wall and stared at the black nothingness beyond the edge of the road. A thousand feet down. He felt sick. He began to tremble.

The cracking whip had finally quieted the mules. They shouldered each other against the inside cliff, tugging fretfully at their jerk line, grunting and wheezing and twitching their enormous ears. The smell of them was pungent on the brittle air.

The stage driver turned balefully to Anders. "That was a two-forty team, mister. A thousand dollars apiece. Jim Birch will take it right outta your hide."

Anders felt a miserable guilt. He saw that the muleskinner had his bandanna out and was rubbing his swinger's eye. "Musta got somethin' in it," he said blandly. "Jumped like he was shot, didn't he?" He looked over his shoulder at them. "I'll give you a lift back to Downieville. Be another stage through in a couple days."

Anders's guilt was swept away on a tide of savage impatience. Two whole days? Jamaica might be gone again. He couldn't wait that long. He couldn't waste another minute.

"Corey," he told the muleskinner, "unhitch six of those mules."

Kettle Corey pointed his red beard to the sky and laughed.

The stage driver was whipping dust viciously from his fancy California pants. "I ain't hitching no jackasses to my coach," he said. "They won't work in anything but a jerk line."

"They'll gee and they'll haw," Anders said. "The Jackass Mail has been using them on the Southern run for years." He pulled out his Walker and pointed it at Kettle Corey. "Unhitch those mules."

The muleskinner looked at the gun a long time. He sneezed. He took the wad of snuff from under his lip and flipped it off into space. Anders watched it go. "I guess that would sting like hell," he said, "if you rubbed it in a mule's eye."

The muleskinner turned around and began unhitching his nigh swinger. Opal moved up beside Anders.

"What did you mean by that?"

"I don't know exactly," he said. "But it was just a small miracle that kept me from going overboard with that first horse."

III

Camptonville was the nearest way station. They got in before dawn, after a maddeningly slow trip with half a dozen mules in a makeshift harness and reins devised from some hemp out of the freight wagons. The relay team replaced

103

the mules and a new front running gear was put on the coach. They got into the transfer point at Grass Valley in early afternoon.

The driver wanted to haul Anders before the division superintendent, but Opal said she would vouch for him. The Wells, Fargo man told Anders that the King's Players were staying at the Beatty Hotel. The clerk at the Beatty said the actors had rooms there but they were probably out at the Montez house on Mill Street. Anders found the cottage, surrounded by a grove of magnificent poplars. He had heard of the exotic Lola Montez, the notorious Countess of Bavaria, intimate of Hugo and Dumas and Liszt, who had created a furor with her Spider Dance in San Francisco and had inexplicably retired to this obscure mining camp with her pet grizzly.

She met him at the door with the bear on a chain. She reminded him instantly of Jamaica, dark, vivid, bringing drama to the slightest gesture. From inside he could hear a pair of men giving a reading. It sounded like something from *Nick of the Woods.*

"Hold, murdering villain! Richard Braxley, forbear!"

"Now, Rowland Forester, I defy thee!"

"Monster, hold . . ."

"Behold the promised bride. Consent to make her mine, or down yon boiling cataract I'll hurl her to destruction. . . ."

Anders asked for Jamaica. Lola Montez studied him with shrewd eyes, then smiled mysteriously and invited him to a sitting room. It was a dark place of spool-turned settees and tabernacle mirrors and rococo marble-topped tables. Lola disappeared, leaving a scent of jasmine in the air. Soon a man came in from the other room. He had a luminous mane of snow-white hair and the bloodshot eyes of a grieving hound. He switched the tails of his rifle-blue outcoat behind him as he made his courtly bow, introducing himself as Parker Innes, the manager of The King's Players. Apparently Jamaica had not told Innes about Anders, for he showed no reaction to Anders's name.

"Madame Montez tells me you seek Jamaica," he said.

"That's right," Anders said.

"Well, Jamaica has many admirers."

"She's with you, isn't she?"

"Alas, alas, I tried to dissuade her, but she and I quarreled. Her humors and her spleens. Perhaps you know. That scene from Febro . . . 'Alack, dear Father,' says Leonora, 'I hope you are not angry.' How that girl can twist such a ravishing face into such ghastly grimace, I do not know. I told her she would simply have to stop mugging and playing to the gallery. Does she think we are a minstrel show . . . ?"

"Innes, are you saying she's gone?"

"Gone, my dear fellow? How you speak. Most assuredly not. We shall be playing Hangtown in a few days and she will be cooled down by then. . . ."

"What does Hangtown have to do with it?"

"Ah . . . you know this Castine? Another one of your ilk. Did you see the nugget he threw to her at the Metropolitan? Big as my fist, sir! Big as my fist."

"Castine, Castine . . . ?"

"Of course, she must have business in mind . . . they say he has money in the American Theater . . . one cannot blame her for looking out after her own interests. But it did hurt, the pains I have taken with her, like a father, like her own father. . . ."

"She's gone to Hangtown with Castine . . . that's what you're saying?"

Innes tucked his thumbs under his satin lapels and leaned back in surprise. "It is unnecessary to shout, dear fellow. If you employ the diaphragm properly, you can shatter their eardrums with a whisper."

Anders found Opal in the California Stage Office still arguing with the driver and the division superintendent. The superintendent had called in the sheriff and was trying to fix responsibility for the lost stage team on Anders. But the sheriff said there was nothing in the statutes to cover it. It was a standard operation, had been necessary on these roads dozens of times before, and, as far as he could see, the conductor's helping to dismantle the coach was tantamount to official sanction by the company. All the fuming superintendent could do was fire Hangtown Charlie and make Anders sign a paper absolving the driver of responsibility. Charlie said he could make more money on his gin anyway and joined Anders and Opal in the waiting room.

The southbound from Marysville would not come through till 3:00 in the morning. They settled down to wait. Anders could feel Opal's eyes on him but he didn't turn to look at her. She said nothing and he was grateful for that. He didn't feel like talking. He didn't know what he felt like. He kept thinking about Castine. He would have been blind not to have considered the possibility of other men. A woman like Jamaica—everywhere she went—it was never any different. But he'd won out over all of them before. He couldn't give up now, so close to the end. . . .

A pair of whiskey drummers came into the waiting room. The fragrance of their cigars made Anders's mouth water. Automatically he fumbled for the cigar cutter dangling from his Dickens chain. Then he made a disgusted sound and stuffed it back inside his coat. He'd been reduced to penny stogies ever since reaching California and he had been without even those for the last few days.

The stage rolled in and they boarded it with the drummers, a miner, a woman who smelled like lilacs and kept her parasol opened in front of her face, and a man in a plug hat and white scissor-tail coat whose trunk announced him as Dr. Magwell Reed, exclusive California dispenser of Dr. Fanestock's Celebrated Vermifuge and Liquid Opeldox, Sherman's Worm Lozenges, Evan's Chamomile Pills, Portuguese Female Pills, and various other indispensable remedies for the cure of ague, dyspepsia, gout, lumbago, St. Vitus's dance, consumption, and green sickness.

Somewhere south of Auburn, Anders fell into a restless sleep. He woke with the morning sun, strong and hot, in his face. Dr. Magwell Reed told him it was almost 10:00 and they had reached their destination. Anders looked out the window to see that they were pulling up a grade into the town.

Officially, he knew, it was Placerville. But the great oak standing at the corner of Main and Caloma had served as courthouse, jury box, and scaffold for so many kangaroo courts that the place was known from the Atlantic to the Pacific as Hangtown. The main thoroughfare rose steeply, following the twisting course of Hangtown Creek. Snow made jagged white streaks in the criss-crossed wheel ruts or lay in dirty drifts against the high curbs. Rickety frame buildings lined both sides of the street. Most of them were unpainted and their clapboard had turned black and rotten in the weather. Every hundred feet the solid rank of buildings was broken by the side streets crawling along the steep mountainsides that lifted behind the first block.

The inevitable freighters stood in long lines at either curb and the hundreds of mules filled the air with an incessant braying. The rank smell of them mingled with the smell of pine smoke and of newly opened earth. Cursing hopelessly, the stage driver threaded his way through the countless excavations in the street. Oblivious to the traffic, men dug in the makeshift mines or sat beside the heaps of earth that had been thrown up, washing the dirt in a rocker to separate it from the gold. It made little impression on Anders. He was gripped by another fever.

The stage halted before a rickety two-story building with a sign on its overhang: Dry Diggings Hotel. Wells, Fargo had their emblem in one of the windows. A pair of agents were carrying gold in iron-bound chests from the office inside to another stage in front. A guard sat on the roof of the coach. He had a tin cup of coffee in his hand, two Colt revolvers in his belt, and a Sharps rifle lying across his lap.

Dr. Magwell Reed was first to leave the Grass

Valley stage, removing his plug hat and helping Opal out with broad theatrical gestures. Anders followed.

"If they're here, they'll probably be staying at the hotel," Opal told Anders. "Dad and I are at Missus Riley's rooming house, just beyond that oak."

There was a plea in her eyes as she looked up at him. Hurried though he was, he took time to say: "Thanks, Miss Mason. Don't worry. I'll keep our bargain."

He turned and went inside. The lobby was narrow, cramped, with a sagging mohair settee jammed against one wall beside the open door of the Wells, Fargo office. A rickety stairway went up the other side. In the alcove beneath it was a roll-top desk with a ledger and a cowbell. He rang the cowbell several times but nobody answered. The ledger was lying open, the date was written at the top of the page, but nobody had registered. He leafed backward. He came to Saturday, February 20th. Only one party had signed in that day. *Mr. and Mrs. Victor Castine.*

He couldn't react for a moment. He simply felt numb. He read it—the whole implication was there, but he felt nothing. He had thought of her with other men and that had been part of the torture. *Mr. and Mrs. Victor Castine. . . .* He felt cold all over and he began to shake, and then he felt hot. He was still shaking and he turned away because he didn't want to see it any more; he didn't want to look at it. He knew Jamaica had not divorced him.

One of the Wells, Fargo agents came back in, dusting his hands off against his tight foxed pants.

"Clerk's out for coffee," he said. "You want a room? I'll sign you up."

"Mister and Missus Victor Castine," Anders said.

"Oh. They're in Two-Oh-Eight. But I think they stepped out a few minutes back."

"A dark woman? A very beautiful, black-haired woman, with a lot of jewelry, who laughs a lot?"

"That's right. She was with him."

Anders walked out. He had a strange, blind feeling. His throat was hot. There was a pressure at his temples. For two years all he had wanted was to see her again. For two years all he could think about was finding her, seeing her again.

Opal was still on the sidewalk waiting for Hangtown Charlie to get her suitcase off the luggage rack. She saw Anders's face. She put her hand to her lips.

"What is it, Mister Anders . . . isn't she here?"

"I've got to go," he said.

"What is it? What happened?"

"Nothing. Don't ask me. I've just got to go, Miss Mason."

"Do you want me to pay your fare back?"

111

There was no change in her face, no accusation in her voice or her eyes. He looked up the street. All he could see were the long lines of mud-spattered mules and three red-shirted muleskinners arguing by a towering Murphy wagon and a man making a wheelbarrow in front of a shack on stilts. He looked down the street. He closed his eyes a minute.

"How far away is this Satan's Keyhole?" he asked.

"If you really don't want to . . ."

"I made the bargain."

"Well, it's quite a distance. You'll have to pack in. Two days."

"I'll go. Right now." *And hope to God Jamaica's gone when I get back,* he thought.

"Hadn't you better talk with Dad first?"

"Right now, Miss Mason."

He had his eyes open and he saw that she was looking at him curiously. She made a helpless motion with one hand, saying: "Very well. Dusty, will you go to Hamsen's and tell them to make up a pack for two men for a week. Bill it to the company. Then try to find Eddie. Tell him to come to Grey's Livery."

The livery stood beyond the venerable gnarled oak at Main and Caloma. There were a barn and haylofts and some rough corrals running down into the creek bottoms. Grey was a heavy, balding man smelling of horse droppings and strong tobacco. Anders helped him round up the animals and saddle them, trying to occupy his mind with the work, trying not to think. There was an ornery mule, still shaggy with his winter coat. There were a buckskin and a paint, mountain horses, big swelling throttles and big rumps.

Opal waited nearby, watching him work. He was almost finished when the little Sydney Duck arrived with a young man. Opal introduced him as Eddie Norris. In the dim light of the big barn Anders got the impression that Norris was young, too heavy, and didn't look rough enough for the dirty red Mackinaw and greasy jeans he wore. He had a cowlick, in the latest fashion, and after shaking hands with Anders he wet his fingers and plastered the cowlick against his forehead. It looked like a nervous habit to Anders, like a man getting out his cigar cutter when he didn't have any cigars to cut.

"I'm glad to meet you, Mister Anders," Eddie said. "I've heard your reputation."

"All of it?"

Norris flushed. "Well . . . uh . . ."

"Eddie wants to be an engineer," Opal said.

Anders acknowledged it with a nod. He asked: "What about the pack?"

"It should be ready by now," Dusty said. "We can pick it up at the general store."

Anders didn't want to go out in the street. He didn't want to take the chance of seeing them.

Mr. and Mrs. Victor Castine. He cleared his throat. "Why don't you go down with the mule and pick it up, Eddie?" he said. "I'll wait here."

"Sure, Mister Anders. Glad to."

Opal was watching Anders, after the young man left. Perhaps his need to be alone showed in his face. "Is there anything else you'll want?" she asked.

"I don't think so."

"Then I'll say good bye now. You'll be in good hands, Mister Anders. Eddie may look a little young, but he knows the country."

She drew one hand from her muff and held it out. He took it. The softness and the warmth of it seemed to go clear through him. He released it quickly. She seemed about to say something else. Then her lips compressed and she turned and walked out. Anders watched her go. He became aware that Grey was looking at him. He turned to see a shrewd glint in the stableman's eyes.

"She's engaged to Eddie Norris," Grey said.

IV

They were in the big country. They left Hangtown behind and moved all morning long into the vast chain of ridge and gorge and peak that rose in unmeasured height against the eastern sky. Snow lay in formless white patches on the chilled

114

rocks of the cañons. Higher up the bigger drifts glittered through stands of fir so green it looked black.

Eddie Norris talked constantly. He had studied engineering in the East, though he had no degree, and now had some complicated idea for improving the hydraulic hoses. He plied Anders with a hundred technical questions. Anders answered in detail, trying vainly to keep his mind off Jamaica. It did no good. Only a corner of him was here. The rest of him was back in that moldy hotel lobby. He wondered why he had come here. It seemed pointless now. Yet anything would be pointless. Maybe part of it had been a sense of obligation to Opal Mason. But there had been a deeper urge. It had been escape—the first at hand—and he had taken it.

They were high on a slope, where the green crowns of the *madroñas* were tilted like umbrellas to shed the rain, when some movement far behind caught his eye. He turned to watch. It came again. A tantalizing impression of something tawny catching the sunlight, flashing like fool's gold in the green sea of distant timber.

At sunset they topped a ridge that must have stood two miles in the air. The horses were laboring and slick with sweat. They halted to let them blow. On all sides lay the mountain world. The deep valleys ahead and behind were beginning to fill with a lilac haze. The tattered banners of red-tinged clouds streamed against the sky and beneath them the most distant chain of ridges was turning to smoke against the solid crimson flame of sunset. The air was so cold it hurt the lungs and it smelled of buckwheat and pitch and pine needles.

A sense of peace touched Anders. Jamaica and all she stood for seemed to fade behind; the long search and the bitter culmination became a dream. There was no other world but this and he could stay up here forever where a man only had to lift his arm to touch the sky. He would never go back.

Something caught his eye again in the distance, and the spell was broken. He turned to look down the long miles of their back trail, where the timber was drowning in a sooty twilight. Eddie saw him looking and turned to watch. It came again, barely visible, the tawny flash deep in the valley.

"Looked like a bear," Eddie said.

"Not a brown bear."

"They've got grizzlies up here."

They made camp in a stand of yellow pine. Camp robbers twittered and quarreled nearby as they poked around in the snow for seeds. Norris's buckskin gave him trouble with the bit. Finally Anders went over to help him get it out.

"You didn't learn that on a drafting board," the young man said.

"I was raised on a farm, Eddie."

"You?"

"Maine," Anders said. "I guess I spent half my life moving rocks. It gave Dad bad kidneys. It twisted him up with rheumatism before I was born. It ruptured him when I was ten. We couldn't get him to stop. The doctor couldn't even make him wear a truss. My old man said that if the good Lord had intended a body to spend his life all laced up that way, He would have put a buckle on instead of a belly button."

Norris laughed.

"Dad said his boys were going to do something better than move rocks all their lives," Anders said. "He even smoked willow bark instead of tobacco. It meant he could save a dollar more a month. It put Jess through law school. And Ned, with his piano . . . they've offered him a European tour."

"I guess your father's proud of you."

"I was in Europe, still studying, when he died," Anders said. He looked off into the night. "It's like a debt you owe somebody, Eddie. Can you understand that? All those rocks he moved for me."

He closed his eyes. It was a debt he hadn't paid. Maybe it was better that the old man had died when he did. Before Mast Hope. Before Chicago. Before Jamaica. . . .

After dinner they turned in. Anders was

exhausted by the long day, but he could not go to sleep immediately. Every time he closed his eyes he saw Jamaica. And there was something else nagging him, a memory, a tawny flash in the timber. The animals were nervous, too. They grumbled and pulled fretfully at their pickets.

Finally he slept. He dreamed of a dark-haired woman whose flashing eyes blinded him and who kept laughing in his face and he went to her crawling on his hands and knees, but when he got there she had changed to a little girl with yellow hair and his hands were imprisoned in a gigantic muff and he could not grasp her and a man who looked like his father said: "She's engaged to Eddie Norris."

He woke up. He was sleeping on his belly and both hands were caught beneath his body. The fire was out and it was intensely cold. But the night had gone. Dawn made a gray tapestry of the timber. The animals were stamping and pulling at their pins and whimpering. They transferred their nervousness to him.

Anders rolled out and put on his coat. He put his gun in his belt and held his right hand under his left armpit to keep it from going numb. He walked out of camp into the timber. The yellow pines were ranked about him like a legion of Roman centurions. Each thick plate of their cinnamon-colored armor was five feet long. He circled camp, hunting for something, he didn't know what. He climbed toward the ridge above, wanting a longer view. He saw a grassy area ahead where *madroñas* grew, big evergreens with twisted limbs and ruddy bark that peeped through the foliage like the arms of an Indian in ambush. To one of the stunted trees a big buckskin horse was hitched.

Anders stopped, still masked by the timber. He pulled his gun. The buckskin cropped peacefully at the *madroña,* unaware of Anders. There was a faint smell on the thin, freezing air, like the distant ferment of a skunk. It was tantalizingly familiar to Anders. It nagged at his memory.

Twigs crackled on one flank. He whirled sharply toward the sound, the gun held rigidly in his hand. Cousin Jack stood ten feet away.

"You looking for somebody?" he asked.

The pungent odor came from his shaggy grizzly-bear coat. The Cornishman had no gun in his mittened hands. Anders did not lower his own weapon.

"That was you following us yesterday," Anders said.

"Was it, guv'ner?"

"Opal wouldn't believe you were in Downieville," Anders said. "She thought I was drunk."

"I wasn't in Downieville, guv'ner."

"Don't you want this bridge to go through, Jack?" Anders asked. The Cornishman did not answer. Finally Anders said: "Get the horse. We'll go into camp."

He accompanied Cousin Jack to the animal. The Cornishman took the reins and they walked back to camp. Norris was just waking up.

"Cousin Jack!" he said. "I thought you were at the bridge."

"I was," the Cornishman said.

Norris saw the gun in Anders's hand and looked surprised. "What is it, Anders? It's all right. This is Cousin Jack. He works for Mister Mason."

"Why don't you get some kindling?" Cousin Jack said. "We'll have breakfast."

While Norris gathered the wood, Cousin Jack found the canteen and poured some water into the top of the flour, making his biscuits in the sack. When the kindling was heaped in the circle of rocks, the Cornishman pulled out a package of English lucifers. He ignited one by pulling it through a piece of folded sandpaper and then lit the fire. Squatted with his back to Anders, most of him masked by the matted bearskin, he looked like some enormous animal. He pulled out a cigar with a pigtail at one end to hold it together. He lit it with another lucifer. The smoke drifted toward Anders and his mouth began to water. He stared hungrily at the cheap New England cigar.

Norris had filled the coffee pot and he set it on the fire. The flame burned his hand and he pulled back with a curse, upsetting the pot and spilling the whole thing on Cousin Jack. The Cornishman stood up and stepped back.

"Eddie," he said mildly, "how many times do I got to tell you to wait for the fire to die down?"

Eddie was holding his burned hand, crimson with embarrassment. "Cousin Jack, I'm sorry. . . . I guess I'm about the clumsiest man in the world."

"Well," Cousin Jack said, "we'll give you another hundred years."

They finished eating before sunrise. Cousin Jack did not actually say so, but Norris assumed that he had been on his way to Hangtown from the bridge and now meant to return with them. Norris made a mess of his blanket roll and it came apart and fell off his horse before they were thirty minutes in the saddle. Anders helped him get it back together properly.

Sunup poured a blinding light into the valley below. Pine needles lay a foot thick on the ground. They gave off an orange-rind smell when the hoofs crushed them, and lifted a dusty resin into the air. Its golden haze swam in the shafts of sunlight that spilled into the cathedral aisles of the forest. They came out of the pines into a meadow and saw a flume held fifty feet in the air by a complex maze of timbers. Norris told Anders that it had carried water from the American River to the You Bet Mine. They followed the flume for an hour before they reached the mine. Along the banks of a dry boulder-strewn creek was a collection of weather-blackened shacks, a broken corral, and mountainous heaps of earth that Norris said were the tailings. He showed Anders the hydraulic monitors, half-covered with snow, still set along the creekbed. Each one had a brass nozzle set on a metal tripod. From the nozzle a rawhide hose led to the flume. When the flume was full, a tremendous head of water could be carried through the hose to the nozzle, enough pressure to wash away a mountainside to get at the gold-bearing gravels underneath. The stream of water then turned the gravel into a series of sluice boxes where the gold fell into the riffles and the gravel was carried on into the tailings at the end.

"The You Bet was washing out ten thousand dollars a day till they went dry," Eddie said.

"What happened?" Anders asked.

"When you get a dozen mines along every mile of river diverting water for their hydraulic operations, you run out of water pretty quick," Eddie said.

Cousin Jack spat disgustedly. "Hydraulickers. If they'd stuck to tunneling, they'd still be in business."

"We'll put 'em back in business," Norris said cheerfully. "Mister Mason says if the Rubicon isn't enough water, he'll take his flumes clear up to Lake Bigler."

Anders was watching Cousin Jack narrowly. "You don't like hydraulicking?" he asked.

"Washing the land away?" The Cornishman's voice was venomous. "You got to pay the earth for her secrets, Anders. Inch by inch, foot by foot, a drop of your blood for every drop of hers. It's her blood you're taking. She broke her back to make them mountains. They came right up through her hide a millions years ago. She burned in hell to make 'em. That magma down there. How hot does it have to be to burn stone? She wasn't done suffering. She had to break her heart to make that ore. Magma cracking wide open as it cooled. Ore flowing into them fissures. Tungsten. Copper. Gold. That's her veins. Ten feet wide. Fifty feet. That's her blood. And you're taking it right out of her heart. The Mother Lode. You can't steal it from her. You can't wash it away and leave her naked. She'll stop you. On way or another she'll stop you."

Anders stared at Cousin Jack, at a loss for words. Yet he knew he should not be surprised. He had visited the tin mines of Cornwall. He had come away with a deep respect for the knowledge of engineering and geology learned patiently through the centuries by these human moles.

"Aren't you forgetting the placers?" he said. "She did that herself."

"Sure she did. Erosion. Thousands of years of it. Lava, ash, mud, tuff, it all got washed away. Some of the gold veins got broken off and went with it. That's what you found in the rivers. She give it free. The biggest fool in the world could come up with a tin pan and get rich. But now that's over. The fools don't know it. They won't stop. They want to wash her hide away right down to her guts."

Norris laughed. "Don't let him bother you, Anders. These hard-rock men are all alike. They'd rather spend a year digging out a mountain that can be washed down in a day."

"I'll remember that," Anders said.

They kept rising. The valley floors were higher and the ridges were higher. It was a world still gripped in winter. Snow was everywhere. It made the air smell wet. It drifted deep in timber and covered the barren areas with a glaring white surface. They had trouble following the threads of rocky ground that meandered through the drifts and half the time the horses were wading to their bellies in snow.

In late afternoon they came to the edge of the world. It was a crack in the plateau that ran east and west beyond sight. Anders gauged it automatically with a surveyor's practiced eye. It must have been a thousand feet deep and a third of a mile wide. He thought of what Cousin Jack had said. The earth breaking her heart a million years ago.

It took Anders's breath away to look over the side. The awesome rock walls were striped with the rich red oxides and blue-gray limestones and lavender sandstones of past geologic ages. Near the bottom the face of the cliff broke off into benches and abutments that tumbled into the milky haze hiding the floor of the cañon. The remnants of a bridge clung to those benches. From the heights the trestles looked as big as a heap of broken matchsticks.

They turned northward along the edge of the chasm. At one rocky promontory Norris halted Anders and pointed to the view. Directly ahead of them the walls of the cliff were overhanging. Their silhouette made the shape of a gigantic keyhole.

Just beyond the keyhole they reached camp. A dozen log cabins stood a few hundred feet back from the gorge. Beyond them a flume came down out of timber. It was not on high trestles like the rotting You Bet flume. It was flat on the ground, a canal twenty feet wide with a wooden floor and sides of whipsawed lumber six feet high. It stopped abruptly at the edge of the gorge.

As the riders approached the cabins, some of the crew came from the doorways. They represented every type Anders had come to know in the diggings. There was a Mexican with a cross around his neck and a knife in his belt. There was a Chileno who wore a yellow vicuña sombrero with little balls of red worsted bobbing all the way around the rim. There was a rigid young man from New England in a clay-stained hat and tight red weskit. Another Sydney Duck like Dusty with the notch of the Australian penal colony in his ear, a Chinese cook who had a fixed smile on his tawny face, and four mountain men in elk-hide leggings and beaded moccasins.

Norris introduced Anders to the foreman. He was named Sluefoot, one of the horde from Pike County, Missouri, who had emigrated to the mines. He was immensely tall, dressed in the archaic surtout and single wool gallus that seemed to be the uniform of the Pikes. He had sharp ears and shaggy brows that came to a peak above his eyes. It gave his snuff-brown face a tilted, pointy look, like the face of a sly satyr.

Anders asked to see the plans. Sluefoot cackled and snapped his gallus with a horny thumb.

"You done left your schoolbooks behind, Mister Engineer. We don't waste time drawin' puny pitchers out here."

Anders was incredulous. "You mean you tried to span that gap without any plans?"

The Pike pulled his triangular ear. "Well, Mister Mason did do some scribblin' around on a couple old paper sacks. Looked like so much chicken scratchin' to me."

"We drove the Cornwall mines a mile down without any maps," Cousin Jack said.

Anders hesitated. This was the first time he'd been with a crew in two years. He looked at the shack, at the edge of the gorge. His indecision angered him. He felt uneasy, inadequate. The crew sensed his confusion and began to stir restlessly.

"Have you got an engineer's shack?" he asked.

Sluefoot pointed to one of the cabins. "Mister Mason bunked there."

"See if you can find those paper sacks," he said. "I'll be down below, looking at the bridge."

Sluefoot ambled unhurriedly toward the shack. Norris led Anders down the trail. Anders glanced questioningly at Cousin Jack. The Cornishman did not follow. Neither did any of the crew. The trail was a narrow ledge hacked from the side of the cliff. A hundred feet down they passed a huge overhanging rock balanced precariously on edge. Eddie slapped it as he went by.

"That's for luck," he said. "They always do it. Mister Mason forgot, the last time he went down."

Anders did not slap the rock. He knew how intensely superstitious most hard-rock men were. No whistling in the mines. Never let a woman in the drifts. If your candle goes out, you go out, too.

They passed from the diamond glitter of

sunlight into the freezing blue shadows of the lower gorge. The trail switched back and forth a dozen times before they reached bottom.

The cañon had been cut by a river originally but there was no water in its boulder-strewn bottom now. A hundred yards from the end of the trail they reached the wreckage of the bridge. One or two of the major uprights were still standing but the bulk of the trestles were strewn like jackstraws across the cañon. Anders studied the standing beams.

"How deep down did you sink these sticks?"

"Ten feet," Norris said. "First time we put it up, Mason didn't think it was necessary to sink them in this bedrock. A flash flood came through here and kicked them right out from under us."

"Anything in the holes?"

"What?"

"Cement, grout, rocks . . . did you put any footing under the uprights?"

"Uh . . . I don't know."

Anders glanced at him. Norris flushed. Anders began kicking at the ground in which the beams had been sunk. What had appeared to be solid rock began to chip and finally he kicked a whole strip from between the harder strips.

"Did Mason really think this was bedrock?" Anders asked. Norris stared at it helplessly. Anders said: "No wonder your trestles came down. This unequal settlement would pull a footbridge apart. I thought Mason was an engineer."

"He's been all over the world. . . ."

His voice was drowned in a roar. It seemed to come from some distant part of the cañon, crashing from one wall to the other, engulfing them. Anders was deafened. He could not tell where the sound came from or what it meant. He knew a moment of pure animal panic.

He saw that Norris was shouting again. But he could not hear him. He saw the young man looking up, pointing at something. Before Anders could turn to look, Norris ran at him. The charging body knocked him off his feet and he pitched backward. Norris went down with him and they rolled across the sandy wash.

As they came to a stop, Anders saw a rock slide sweep over the spot where he had been standing. In its midst, bouncing, tumbling, crashing, was the enormous boulder Eddie had slapped on the way down.

It roared across the cañon, smashing the wrecked trestles to tinder, and finally came to a stop in the sand a hundred yards from the two men. The dust settled about them and the echoes rolled down the cañon and stopped. Anders got up, giving Norris a hand.

"Thanks, Eddie. You'll make an engineer yet."

Norris grinned sheepishly, brushing himself off. Anders looked up the side of the cliff. He saw

Sluefoot above them. The man was on a section of the trail below where the rock had been. He had some brown wrapping paper in his hand.

"You all right?" he called. "I told 'em all their slappin' would loosen that rock sooner or later."

Anders did not answer. There was a man above Sluefoot, looking down at them. Anders could not tell if he was on the trail or on the edge of the cliff. The sun made a golden glitter against his long grizzly-bear coat.

V

They went back to Hangtown. There was nothing more Anders could do at the Keyhole. One look at the wreckage and the bottom of the chasm had told him what was necessary. Cousin Jack went with them. It was a tense trip. Anders slept with his gun under his hand and always rode behind Jack on the trail.

It was not exactly new to him. There was always some sorehead in a gang who caused trouble sooner or later. He had worked beside more than one man who had threatened to get him. But this was insidiously different. There was too much under the surface. He could not figure out the Cornishman. Sometimes he thought he was getting a glimpse of the man's motives, but it was always too brief, too elusive.

And Eddie Norris seemed supremely oblivious to the undercurrents of hostile tension that remained between the two men all the way back to town.

They arrived after dark. Main Street was lined with the jagged yellow blossoms of torches. It was crowded with the shadowy passage of men, threading their way through the labyrinth of coyote holes that pocked the streets, turning the snowdrifts to slush beneath their feet. Their sound was like a sullen surf, broken now and then by a startling gust of laughter or a hoarse shout. They dismounted at the stable and called for Grey.

"We could eat first, if you like," Norris told Anders. "I'm starved."

Anders was looking down toward the Dry Diggings Hotel. He couldn't help it.

"Let's see Mason," he said savagely. "Let's get it over with."

They went to the boarding house just beyond the spreading hang tree at the corner of Main and Caloma. A dozen people were at the long table in the dining room and the smell of sourdough biscuits and green apple pie filled the room. But neither Opal Mason nor her father was in evidence. Mrs. Riley told Anders that Mason had been taking his meals in his rooms. The three men went upstairs.

Opal Mason answered their knock. She had a quilted dressing robe over her shirtwaist. Its deep wine color made the flesh of her throat startlingly white. She had unpinned her hair and it lay like thick coils of honey against her shoulders. A pleased flush touched her cheeks as she saw Anders.

"We're back," Norris said.

For another moment she did not take her eyes off Anders's face. Then, almost reluctantly, she looked at Norris.

"Of course, Eddie," she said. It sounded indulgent, almost motherly. Norris frowned and looked down at his feet. It made Anders think of a little boy and a schoolmarm. Opal touched Cousin Jack on the arm. "You and Eddie better stay in here. Dad isn't up to a crowd yet."

She turned and crossed the room. It apparently sufficed for her bedroom as well as the parlor. A narrow mohair settee against one wall had been made up with blankets and a pillow.

Cousin Jack had closed the living room door. He stood with his back against it, holding his bowler hat in both hands, watching Anders with sullen eyes.

Anders followed Opal into the other room. It was crudely furnished with a gilt mirror, a cracked marble washstand, tattered hooked rugs. The milky prisms of a Sandwich lamp cast a yellow glow over the man lying in a button-turned bed.

He had a long, gaunt-boned, Jacksonian face.

He had a tangle of unkempt hair and Opal's thick brows, shaggier, dead-white. His eyes were deeply sunken from long sickness and his cheeks had a sucked-in look. Age gave a furred look to the edges of his face. The flesh lay, loose and gray, against his neck like the wattles of a turkey. When Opal introduced them, Mason waved at a whiskey bottle beside his half-finished dinner on the side table.

"Pour Mister Anders some of that coffin varnish, honey, and then he can give me the facts and figures."

The booming voice, coming from such a gray and suffering face, surprised Anders. He said: "Thanks, Mister Mason, but my stomach's too empty for a drink. Our business won't take too long anyway." Anders hesitated. Then he said: "I can't build your bridge."

Mason lay heavily against the pillows, lowering his head till his eyes were invisible beneath the ragged white hedges of his brows. "You don't think it can be done?"

"I didn't say that. I just can't do it for you."

"Then you think it can be done?"

"Let's not get into technicalities."

"Damn my eyes," the old man said. "I thought I was getting me an engineer. I thought my brother knew men. Colonel Mason said you were the best damn' engineer on the railroad, but you'd gone to hell over some woman . . ."

"Dad," Opal said. "Don't excite yourself. You know that the doctor . . ."

"Hell with the doctor." Mason struck the bed, glaring at Anders. "I don't think there was a woman at all. With them lake-front trestles you'd just come up against a job that was too big for your britches. You knew it was a-goin' to be the Mast Hope bridge all over again and you couldn't face it. . . ."

"What do you know about trestles?" Anders interrupted savagely. "You spend all your life digging holes in the ground and then you think you can come up and try to span a cut like the Keyhole with abutments out of the Stone Age. . . ."

"What's the matter with my abutments?"

"Nothing a little oscillation wouldn't wreck. What made you think you didn't have to sink the piers?"

"You must've looked at the first job. I dug holes the last two times. . . ."

"Without any footing in them."

"I had bedrock."

"I could kick it out with one foot. You had enough unequal settlement there to pull down a city."

"What d'you textbook jockeys know about settlement?"

"I'd know enough to quit trying it with trestles after they came down three times. Your formation's too treacherous. Where you'd find bedrock for one abutment, you'd have nothing but strata for the other."

"What'd you do? Hold it up with balloons?"

"Have you thought of suspension?"

"Great Uncle Harry!" Mason beat the bed. "Great Uncle Harry, did you hear that? And no decent cable this side of New York."

"There was some Birmingham on the docks at Frisco. It looked like number nine and it was tagged to a shipping company in Sacramento."

"Suppose we could bid them out of it? Where would we spin it?"

"Why spin? Some of the best bridges in Europe are hung with parallel wires."

Mason sagged back into the pillows. His eyes were closed and there was a triumphant smile on his face.

"I thought you'd come up with something worthwhile."

Anders realized then how the old man had deliberately goaded him. He couldn't help smiling. Opal smiled. Then they were all laughing.

"Would you ask Missus Riley to send up a meal," Mason told his daughter. "This man looks like he didn't even stop to eat dinner, and we've got a long conference ahead of us."

"Dad, haven't you had enough excitement . . . ?"

"It's a-goin' to be very calm from here on in,

Daughter, very calm and gentle. I won't raise my voice above a whisper."

Opal shook her head helplessly, glanced at Anders, and left. As the door closed, Mason beckoned to Anders. When Anders stood beside the bed, the old man spoke in a low voice.

"Do you really think I don't know bedrock when I see it?"

"That's what puzzled me, Mister Mason. A man that's dug as many tunnels as you . . ."

"I was there when they struck it. I made the surveys and set the stakes out myself."

"Then somebody moved your stakes," Anders said. The old man looked up at him sharply, his eyes dark, disturbed. Anders asked: "Are there any interests around here that might oppose the water company?"

"Interests? What interests?"

"A rival water company."

Mason snorted. "Not a whit. You can't keep that kind of operation quiet. Do you know how big they'd have to capitalize? We'd hear about it from Frisco. They'd be putting up their flumes. All the Lode would know."

"Well, the miners . . ."

"Hell, every miner from here to Lake Bigler is waiting for this water like a thirsty dog in August. They ain't in business without it, Anders. Half of 'em got money in it themselves. The other half are on my crews."

Anders glanced at the door. "Do you know how Cousin Jack feels?"

Mason looked up, surprised. Then he snorted. "*Agh*, I know. The old coot wants to go back to tunneling. He thinks this hydraulic mining is the devil's own doing. But it's just the grumbling of a congenital lode miner, Anders. Don't pay any heed."

Anders walked to the window. He hated to plant suspicion of an old friend in this man's mind. Yet he could not overlook what had happened.

"I'll tell you something, Mister Mason. I've been hunting my wife for two years. . . ."

"So we heard."

"Cousin Jack was in Downieville. He got to me right after your daughter did. He didn't want me to come back here with Opal. He tried to stop me with a gun."

Mason did not answer. The only sound in the room was the snapping of the fire in the soapstone stove. Anders turned. Mason was staring fixedly at him. Feverish spots of color had come to the old man's cheeks and one of his hands had knotted up the bedspread. Anders continued.

"Our stage was blocked on the Mountain House grade by a sixteen-hitch freighter, Mister Mason. The only way we could get around was to take the coach apart and carry it past. While I was leading one of the stage horses past, the freight mules went crazy. They shoved the horse off and

I almost went with it. I think the freighter rubbed snuff in his lead mule's eye. The freighter's name is Kettle Corey. He works for an outfit called Sacramento Shippers."

Mason was staring at him. The name brought no recognition to the old man's eyes. Impatiently Anders went on.

"Cousin Jack didn't go with us when we went below to look at the bridge. That good-luck rock came loose and started a slide. I would have been buried if it hadn't been for Eddie." Mason made a rattling sound deep in his throat. "Doesn't all this add up to something?" Anders asked.

Mason struck the bed. "Get Jack in here."

"Then it does mean something."

"You hear me? Get Jack!"

Anders crossed and opened the door. There were two new people in the parlor, talking with Opal. A handsome man with a single white streak through his black hair and a woman in musty black who kept a crumpled lace handkerchief pressed to her mouth. Opal turned toward Anders, smiling.

"Mister Anders, this is Mister and Missus Victor Castine."

Anders stared at the stooped, gray-faced woman. In a hollow voice, he said: "Mister and Missus Victor Castine?"

"Victor," Mrs. Castine said, "is there a window open? I feel a draft."

Anders turned to the man. "Jamaica . . . ?"

"Oh, she stayed at the hotel," Victor Castine said. He was looking curiously at Anders. "What is it, man?"

Anders did not answer. He was already going past them. The Macassar oil perfuming Victor Castine's hair was so strong that Anders could still smell it when he was out in the hall.

VI

There was a balding clerk dozing at the desk in the Dry Diggings Hotel. Anders went upstairs without waking him. There was no lamp in the second floor hallway. Anders remembered that the Wells, Fargo agent had said the Castines had 208. He struck a match and held it to the first door. There was no number. The match went out and in the darkness he could see that only one door in the hall had a streak of light beneath it.

His palms were sweating as he went toward it. He stopped. He lifted his hand to knock. His throat ached and there was a burning sensation in his eyes. He dropped his hand. He bowed his head and closed his eyes. With a soft curse he lifted his hand again and knocked.

"Yes? Who is it?"

Her voice. Her strange, cultivated, stage voice.

He heard a stirring inside. The door was open a crack.

"Jamaica!"

She pulled the door wide. Her lips were parted but there was no surprise on her face. In one hand she held her engraved pepperbox. She smiled, her dazzling smile.

"Come in, Glenn," she said.

She backed into the room as he entered. He shut the door and stood with both hands behind him still on the knob. He wasn't going to make a fool of himself. He wasn't going to go to her like a callow boy and try to take her in his arms and have her evade him and leave him standing foolishly in the middle of the room.

She wore the Madonna hairdressing he had first seen in New Orleans, the lacquered braids drawn back over the pink ears in a hair net. She was wearing the last dress he had given her, a green satin bodice and the strip of moiré antique in the long sleeves—and the fantastic brooch the French count had thrown on stage in Chicago. She was already lifting her chin and turning her face so her eyes would catch the light. They flashed like the diamond eardrops turning and twisting against her neck.

She seemed to become aware of the pepperbox in her hand. She looked at it and smiled wryly. "Excuse me," she said. She put the little four-barreled gun on the armoire. "These mining camps aren't exactly the drawing room at the Union Place."

The lamp gave off the faint incense of Porter's fluid. It could not compete with her scent. Her presence filled the room. Shimmering silks and glistening brocades spilled in a prodigal cascade from the open trunks under the window. Her velvet jewel case was overturned on the armoire. The ivory top was littered with glittering stones. Handfuls of $2 garnets mingled in a senseless heap with a pearl choker worth $4,000 and the huge ruby stomacher the Indian prince had given her in New Orleans.

He felt like a bumpkin, staring at her like a fool. "Jamaica . . ."

"Won't you sit down, Glenn?" she asked. Her gowns and robes covered every chair in the place. She pulled one off the haircloth settee to make room, dropping it carelessly to the floor. "Can I give you a drink?"

"Jamaica, can't you stop acting for once? It's been two years. Surely you didn't know I was here. . . ."

"As a matter of fact, I did. I went with the Castines a few days ago when they first went to meet Garrett Mason. Mason told us he'd hired you and you were already out at Satan's Keyhole. Then the Wells, Fargo agent told me a man had been here asking for me, a big blond man with a scar on his chin who charged out like a mad lion."

"I thought . . . I didn't know . . . I saw it in the register, dammit, Mister and Missus Victor Castine . . ."

She pouted and frowned at him. She always pouted when she didn't understand something. Then the implication reached her. She threw back her head and laughed. He turned his back and walked to the window. How could she laugh? She must know what it had done to him.

The laughter stopped and he heard the hiss of moiré sleeves as she moved up behind him. "I'm sorry, Glenn. Dear, darling, I'm sorry."

She put one hand on his shoulder. He turned around. She tried to step back but it was too late. He kissed her. She tried to turn her head aside but his lips were already on hers. It forced her head back and arched her whole body against his.

For a moment she fought him. Then she made a low moaning sound. Her hands went behind his head, the fingers digging into the yellow mane of hair, and her lips opened beneath his. Her eyes were open but they were out of focus, blind, a look he knew so well.

"Glenn, Glenn, Glenn . . ."

"Jamaica, I'm taking you back, we've got to start again. We've got to do it different. We're no good apart and you know it, neither of us. . . ."

She twisted free. His arms had relaxed as he talked and he could not stop her in time. She

142

walked across the room with her back to him. He followed her, reaching out.

"Jamaica . . ."

"No, Glenn . . . no!"

She turned again, walking down to the other end of the armoire. He stood where she had left him. Her back was still turned but he could see that her hands were up to her face.

"At least you aren't acting now. This is how you really feel and you can't deny it."

"How do you know what I feel? I've kissed a hundred men since Chicago."

"Not like that."

She did not answer. He circled in front of her. She had taken her hands from her face. Her eyes looked wet.

"Jamaica, what do you want?" he asked. "If it's all my fault, I'll admit it. There'll never be any talk about money again. I swear it. You can have it any way you want it, anything you want. We don't even have to go back. There's plenty of theaters for you here. The camps in summer, Frisco in the winter. There's a job for me here, too."

"Satan's Keyhole? That will last about as long as the Erie, or the Central. . . ."

"You know why that happened," he said. "I won't let it happen this time. Mason's talking about shares as well as a salary. It will mean real money when the water company gets operating."

"That wouldn't help. We're two different kinds of people, Glenn. You traveled ten thousand miles for nothing. Weren't the papers enough for you?"

"Papers?"

"The divorce papers, the notice," she said. He stared so blankly at her that she asked: "Didn't you get them? I filed over a year ago."

He couldn't answer for a moment. He had to take a deep breath. At last, in a dull voice, he said: "How could I get them . . . jumping around half the world?"

"Well, you know now."

"They aren't final, are they?" he said. He seized her arms. "Give it another chance, Jamaica . . . one more try . . . you've got to. . . ."

"Glenn, the Castines are due back any minute. Do you want them to walk in on this? Shall we make a scene for them?" She tore free, whirling to pick up the little pepperbox. "Shall I shoot you again, like New York, or scar your face up some more with a perfume bottle? Shall we do that?"

Now she was acting again. It was the high, shrill voice she affected on the stage. Automatically she had tossed her head to just the correct angle, so that lamplight flashed in her eyes.

Anders was trembling. There was a bitter taste in his mouth and his face was white. He walked to her and tore the little gun out of her hand and flung it across the room. For a moment he thought he would strike her. Then he turned around and walked out.

VII

It was bitterly cold outside. A wind swept Main Street, bringing with it the frozen touch of snow and ice from the high country. Anders stood on the sidewalk shivering violently, waiting for the chill shock to drive the bitter sense of defeat from him. But it would not help. He put his hands in his pockets and walked up the rickety plank sidewalk, unaware of the crowd that jostled him and threw him against the wall. He passed a saloon and the pine scent in the air was replaced by the reek of cheap whiskey.

He stood a moment staring at the batwing doors and the shadowy figures in the smoky light beyond. He needed to strike out at something. He needed to get roaring drunk and fight every man in the place till one of them knocked him out.

He had done it often enough before in a futile attempt to lose the sense of helplessness, the insidious frustration, the feeling of incompetence that always came with their battles. Stinking drunk every night in New York or Boston or Chicago, brawling with men he never knew and never remembered. It was what had happened to his figures on the Mast Hope job. A man couldn't drain his energies with the constant round of theater parties or spend his life in the half world of hangovers and marital battles and expect his mathematics to hold up. It had certainly lost him his Illinois Central job. Colonel Mason was so dead-set against his men drinking on the job that he had even put a ban on the railroads carrying liquor.

How could a man debase himself like that? How could he crawl? Where was the flaw? He'd never doubted his manhood before. He could hold his own with any of them on the job. He'd never felt incompetent with the best of them, even Colonel Mason. He could match wits in the board rooms or set rails all day with the Irish micks, it didn't matter. He could stand up to any Missouri Pike in a brawl or drink any Bohunk teamster under the table. In his world they had taken his measure and it had been good enough. And the moment he stepped into her world . . .

A man came out of a saloon. He was no taller than Anders but there was so much muscle in his shoulders that it made him seem twice as big. It gave him a grotesque top-heavy appearance. Anders recognized the shape before the man swung into the light. It was Cousin Jack.

He saw Anders and stopped a foot away. Jack had his round hat on and his bearskin collar was turned up behind his neck. The dim light accented the etched look of his face. His blue eyes were glazed and his lips were slack and wet. He wiped them with the back of his hand.

"I won't forget that, Anders. I won't ever forget that."

"I thought Mason should know what was happening."

"I was an orphan, Anders. When I was eight years old, I went down in them Cornwall mines as a nipper. I didn't have no father and no mother and no sister and no brother. I slept in a packing box at the edge of town and I spent my waking life down in them holes. By the time I was eighteen I was dying of miner's con. Mister Mason found me down there. He took me out of the holes and kept me with him till I was well. He made me his engineer and we started digging again, right. We went to Peru and Bolivia. We went to France and Italy. For twenty years I've been with Mister Mason. Do you think I'd pull that bridge down on him?"

"I didn't say that."

"You might as well have said it. You put it in Mister Mason's mind. He wouldn't say it. But he's got it there like a worm crawling around in him, and you put it there."

"What about Kettle Corey?" Anders asked. "Is he in this with you?"

The Cornishman blinked. He was swaying,

bleary-eyed. The smell of whiskey was raw and stinging on his breath.

"In what with me?" he asked stupidly.

"Kettle Corey didn't just happen to be on the Mountain House Grade with that freight outfit, did he?" Anders asked. "First you try to stop me in Downieville, and when you miss, Kettle Corey shows up and I almost got kicked off a cliff. What does it add up to, Jack?"

The Cornishman swayed so close his chin almost struck Anders. "I don't know nothing about Kettle Corey. All I know is Mister Mason has got to stop. This thing is ruining him. It's taken all his money, and if he don't quit, it'll take him, too. The next time that bridge comes down, it'll kill him. I knew what you were the first time I saw you in Downieville. I panned you down to bedrock and there wasn't a bit of color showing. I won't let some drunken wreck come along and kill Mister Mason."

"That's a very tender sentiment. Kettle Corey is just the fragile, sensitive kind of soul to share it with you."

Cousin Jack made a rumbling sound. "You're getting out tonight, Anders."

"I don't have the fare."

"I'll give it to you."

"I won't take it."

Cousin Jack put a hand on his gun. "You'll take it."

Anders waited. He wanted Jack to go ahead. He wanted to fight. He had to get his hands on something. Then the mood was gone. He felt empty, sick. He didn't even take his hands out of his pockets.

"Don't pull that gun, Jack," he said. "You and I don't have anything to fight about."

He turned and walked up the street. He heard Jack shout after him, something drunken, unintelligible. He didn't turn around. If that Cornishman ever shot him, it wouldn't be in the back.

VIII

With his hands in his pockets, Anders moved morosely up and down the street. He passed the door of the Riley boarding house a dozen times, the conflict gnawing at him. He was a fool to stay on, a fool to try again. Hadn't the meeting proved anything? There was nothing left for him. There was not even anything left in Jamaica. So cool, so distant, talking to a stranger. That's what they were, strangers. They had been strangers from the beginning.

Yet if she went back to the King's Players, she'd be in the Lode country all summer playing one camp or another. He had to see her enough, that was all. How could he tell from just one meeting? It was a pose. She was acting. She was always acting. He could break through. He could see what she really felt. All he needed was the time.

He pulled out his cigar cutter and fished absently in his empty pockets. Then he cursed and looked down at the cutter dangling uselessly at the end of the Dickens chain. He stuffed it back in his pocket and went into the boarding house.

Opal answered his knock. The Castines were still in the living room. Mrs. Castine sat on the haircloth sofa with her Manila shawl carefully shielding her neck and her lavender handkerchief crumpled in one hand. Victor Castine rose as Anders entered.

"Well, Mister Anders, did you find the creature of your dreams?"

"Dreams?"

"I will admit I've seen men react that way before, but mostly it was in the theater. After her last performance at San Francisco it took three hours to clear the stage door."

"Jamaica didn't tell you?" Anders asked.

"About what?" Castine asked. There was a blank look on his face. Anders realized Opal had not told them, either. He glanced at her. She made a helpless little gesture with one hand. There was a look of compassion on her face. He knew a moment of warmth for a girl sensitive enough to try to spare his feelings that way.

"I'm no stage door Johnny, Mister Castine," he said. "I'm Jamaica's husband."

Castine glanced at Opal in complete confusion. He cleared his throat. He smoothed his carefully groomed hair with one pale forefinger.

"Well . . . uh . . . Anders . . ."

"I knew that girl had something on her soul," Mrs. Castine said. "No wonder my Glauber's Salts wouldn't relieve her."

"How long have you known her?" Anders said.

"We saw a lot of her in San Francisco last winter," Castine said. "Then we ran into her again on our way through Grass Valley. She was having trouble with Parker Innes. We invited her to join us. I spend a lot of time at the mine while I'm up here and Laurette gets lonely . . ."

"Stop prattling, Victor," Laurette Castine said. "Mister Anders certainly doesn't want to discuss his intimate affairs with strangers." The sharp tone of her voice was totally incongruous in the hesitant, apprehensive mouse Anders had seen in her up to now. He glanced at her and she pulled her shawl fussily about her shoulders, saying: "Opal tells us you are an engineer, and saw the Keyhole."

Anders looked questioningly at Opal. The girl said: "The Castines have a natural interest, Mister Anders. Victor is on the board of the Mason Water Company. He's also chairman of the board for the Golden Monte. It's the biggest mine in

Placerville. It stands to gain more than any other company by the completion of our flumes."

"Mason told me you were reluctant to take the job," Victor Castine said. "Don't you think it can be done?"

"On the contrary, I think it can."

"How?" Laurette Castine asked.

Anders looked at her again. The pasty, self-indulgent look was gone from her face. She was watching him narrowly and her eyes held a hawk-like sharpness.

"Suspension," he said.

Laurette Castine shook her head disgustedly. "It would take a year to get the wire from Boston."

Anders frowned at her, surprised at such immediate technical considerations from a woman. "I saw some Birmingham rusting on the beach at Frisco," he said. "It was tagged to Sacramento Shippers."

"Sacramento?" Castine asked.

"Yes," Anders said. "What do you know about them?"

"He knows nothing about them," Laurette Castine said, "except that they're a decrepit, nefarious little one-horse outfit that defaulted on three contracts to supply the Golden Monte with ore wagons. If they left some wire on the beach at Frisco, I'm not surprised. They wouldn't have the money to pay for a pound of nails."

"Perhaps you know Kettle Corey," Anders said.

"Who?"

"A giant, built like a tub, uses snuff . . . ?"

"One of their teamsters?" she asked. "I believe I've seen him. I could never get close enough to speak with such ruffians. The stench would simply destroy my sinuses."

"If Sacramento is so hard up, maybe they'll be glad to have the wire taken off their hands," Anders said.

"Assuming we get the wire, Mister Anders, you'll never find the mechanics for such a job. The kind of experts you need would have to be imported."

"It's funny," Anders said. "Mister Mason tried to argue me into the job. Now you're trying to argue me out of it."

"Garrett Mason is a dreamer," Laurette Castine said. "The time has come to face facts. We're desperate for that water, Mister Anders, but we can't take a chance on another failure. Present us with a feasible plan and we'll give you a contract right now."

Anders looked toward the closed bedroom door. Opal said quickly: "Dad's asleep, Mister Anders. I think he's had enough excitement for one day." She turned to the other woman. "Dad thinks Anders can do it, Laurette. Why don't you give him a chance?"

Laurette Castine closed her eyes and pinched

the bridge of her nose. "Victor, did you bring my headache powders?"

"They're at the hotel, dear. We'd better go back." Castine turned to Anders. "We'll talk again. Perhaps you can give us more details."

Opal saw them to the door. She closed it and returned to Anders. Her cheeks were flushed; there was an excited shine to her eyes.

"Dad gave me a written authorization for the wire. Eddie can be in San Francisco by Saturday," she said. Anders looked dubiously at the door. Opal made an impatient sound. "They've been very discouraged . . . you can understand . . . and Laurette's such a hopeless pessimist, but Dad can win them over. We can't afford to wait, Glenn. Just say the word . . . Eddie can take the stage out tonight."

He hesitated, thinking about Jamaica. Then he grew angry. Why did she have to be considered in this? "All right," he said. "You've got an engineer."

IX

Anders and Mason went into the contract the next morning. Anders was to get a $100 a month cash, ten shares of Mason Water for every week on the job, a bonus of a hundred shares for finishing and another bonus of a hundred more for getting

154

it done by March 15th. The shares were worth $2 apiece now. But Mason showed Anders the commitments from every mine in the area. The prices they were willing to pay for the water convinced Anders that Mason was not dreaming when he expected the stock to take a fabulous jump as soon as the water reached the diggings.

Anders got a week's advance on his salary for his personal needs. The first thing he did was buy a hundred supers at the general store. He kept six of them out and had the rest packed in a box and sent to the livery stable with his other purchases. Then he found a bench near the hang tree and sat there smoking a whole cigar down. Wreathed in so much fragrant smoke that he could hardly see the hotel whenever he looked down the street, he spent the time trying to get up the courage to see Jamaica again. He knew he would have to stay on the job a week or ten days once he got there. But the thought of her brought the old indecision, the apprehensions.

Finally he could take no more pleasure in his cigar. He flung the butt from him and stalked down to the hotel. The clerk told him that Jamaica had gone with the Castines out to the Golden Monte. Depressed and frustrated, he went back to the livery stable.

Cousin Jack was waiting for him there with Dusty. Anders did not like the idea of a two-day trip with the sullen Cornishman, but it took the curse off to have the Sydney Duck along. Despite his evil background Dusty was a good-humored little man, with a way of poking sly jokes at Cousin Jack, and he had never shown Anders anything but cheerful acceptance.

They moved into the big country with Dusty chattering all day like a squirrel and Cousin Jack riding in hostile silence. Anders put his naked Walker Colt inside his blankets that night. He woke at daybreak to see Cousin Jack not three feet away, towering blackly against the pearly sky, staring at him.

Dusty was hopping around in his red long johns trying to get a fire started. He sent a bright glance at Cousin Jack's side whiskers, silvery and brittle with hoar frost. "Why don't you shave those Piccadilly weepers off, Jack? Someday they'll freeze up and slit your throat when you turn your head."

To Anders's surprise, Cousin Jack grinned. He lumbered over and picked up the coffee pot, giving Dusty an affectionate shove. "Get that fire going, you little murderer. I'll put another notch in your ear."

They reached Satan's Keyhole near evening of the second day. Anders could hear the commotion before they got into camp. The whole crew was gathered around something in the compound and their shouts rolled down the timber aisles in reverberating echoes. From the height of his saddle Anders could look over their heads. In their midst he saw the Chinese cook dancing around a mule. His queue was tied to the mule's tail and the mule was kicking and bucking wildly. The cook had all he could do to stay on his feet and keep from getting kicked in the face. The mule was dragging him around in circles and the crowd surged back and forth to escape the lashing hoofs, hooting and catcalling wildly.

Anders rammed his horse against the men, breaking a path through them. When he was inside, he swung off and pulled the breechloader from his saddle scabbard.

"Don't shoot 'em both!" some Pike called. "That's a good Missouri mule."

Anders circled the mule till he could catch its halter. The mule bucked and lashed out with its hind hoofs. Anders cracked it across the tender muzzle with his rifle barrel. The mule brayed and kicked. Anders cracked it on the nose again. The mule kicked. Anders struck once more. This time the mule did not kick.

"Dusty!" Anders yelled. "Hold this mule. Let him kick again and I'll take away your slung-shot."

The Sydney Duck scampered in to grab the mule's halter. Anders gave him the rifle. The mule rolled its eyes, hee-hawing. Dusty showed him the rifle. The mule settled down.

Anders kept his hand on the animal till he got to

157

its rump. The Chinese was shaking and weeping from sheer exhaustion. Anders untied his queue and took him by the arm, leading him away from the mule. It was like holding up a bag of bones.

"Who did it?" Anders asked. "Who tied you up like that?" The Chinese looked at him with wide eyes. He made a strange croaking sound.

"Tin Pan can't talk," Dusty said. "They had Chinese moving day down at Hangtown. Some Pike cut out his tongue."

Anders stared incredulously at the Chinese. Tin Pan nodded, making the unintelligible sounds again.

"Point them out," Anders said. "The men who did this." Tin Pan began to quake and pull away. Anders gripped his arm tighter. "Take it easy. They won't touch you again. You've got to tell me."

The man would not point. But his wide, shining eyes circled the crowd and stopped unmistakably on a dark-faced man from Chile. The Chileno shook his head, the worsted balls dancing around his hat brim.

"I no do, no, I no do. . . ."

"He done it," one of the trappers said.

Anders looked at the trapper. "Who else?"

The trapper pointed a scarred hand at one of the Missouri Pikes. "Leeper done it."

Anders released the Chinese. He looked at the Pike named Leeper and at the Chileno. "You're fired. I want you out of this camp."

158

Sluefoot stepped out of the crowd. The sharp-faced foreman stood, sway-backed and arrogant, snapping the single gallus that held up his linsey-woolsey pants and making a shiny bulge in one cheek with his chaw.

"You can't do that, Mister Engineer. We're short-handed as it is. The boys jist got tired waitin' and had to have a little fun. . . ."

"That's right," Leeper said. "You can't fire us. We only take orders from Mister Mason."

Anders walked over to Leeper. He could see a sly, grinning belligerence enter the Pike's face, could see the man's towering body shift weight as he set himself. Anders stood a foot from the Pike, arms at his sides, looking into the man's tobacco-colored eyes. The crowd grew hushed, waiting. As Anders did nothing, he could see the confusion enter the Pike's eyes. When the pressure grew too much, the Pike started to speak.

"Well, Mister Engineer . . ."

Anders kicked him in the shin. The man howled and started to bend forward. Anders hit him in the belly. It snapped Leeper almost double. Anders hit him at the base of the skull. It put Leeper on the ground.

They had been heavy, driving blows, with all Anders's weight behind them. Leeper was stunned and he lay without moving on the ground. Anders stood beside him, waiting for him to recover. He looked at the Chileno and the Chileno started edging away. The crowd shifted restlessly. Sluefoot studied Anders with narrow, tilted eyes, but said nothing. At last Leeper groaned and stirred. He began to retch feebly and turned over on one elbow to be sick. When he had finished, and some of the film was gone from his eyes, Anders said: "I want you out of this camp in five minutes." He turned to the crowd, raising his voice. "The next one to touch the Chinaman will get spread-eagled on a wheel and horsewhipped."

Anders took his rifle from a gaping Dusty, got his horse, and led it to the engineer's shack. The cook followed, watching the men fearfully. Anders told him he could sleep in the shack if he wanted, and the man grinned and made grateful signs with his hands.

One of the trappers angled toward the shack. His face looked young but it was fearfully gaunt and half hidden by a matted black spade beard. He wore elk-hide leggings, black with grease, and a shirt made from a red Hudson's Bay four-pointer.

"I liked that," he said. "Those Pikes are the orneriest critters on the face of the earth."

"What's your name?" Anders asked.

"Jesse Barton."

Anders shook his hand. "How do you trappers fit in here?"

"You'll find a lot of mountain men in the

diggings, Anders. I been trying to make a stake to bring my wife and kids from Saint Looey. Two years at trapping left me dead broke. I tried pick and panning along the American. Got a little stake but not near enough. Then Garrett Mason come along with his proposition. If we'd invest our money and our time, we'd share in the company's profits."

"You should be able to fetch your family with that," Anders said. "The way they seem to need water down in the valley a few shares should make a man rich."

Barton nodded. He pulled thoughtfully at his beard. "What are your plans about the patrol?"

"Patrol?"

"Mister Mason kept someone riding the flume all the time. Since he left, it sort of petered out. Nobody's been on patrol for a week."

Anders looked at the flume. The wooden aqueduct, with its high plank sides, had been staked flat against the ground. Stained and blackened by weather, it crawled down out of the timber and crossed the boulder-studded bench and ended at the very edge of the abyss.

"How many of you trappers here?" Anders asked.

"Four."

"You know the mountains better than the rest. How about taking the patrol over permanently? I'll talk to Mister Mason about a bonus."

Barton grinned with boyish eagerness. "Suits me."

"Work it out among you then. Just so somebody's on watch all the time."

As Barton crossed toward the other trappers, Anders looked at the camp. The crew had broken up, drifting back to their cabins and campfires. Leeper and Chileno were moving away on a pair of mangy, spavined horses, their gear loaded carelessly behind their saddles. At the edge of camp they halted, looking back at Anders. Leeper said something. Chileno nodded. The little balls of worsted dangling from his hat brim bobbed and danced. Anders watched the two men ride off until they were dying shadows in the twilight.

The next day Anders shook down his crew. He rooted out the troublemakers and the slackers and put them in a group apart, giving them the menial jobs around camp where they would not affect the important work. He interviewed the others and found the ones with some construction and mechanical background. He put them to work on the construction of a pier at the edge of the gorge. He gave Cousin Jack no definite duties. The man lounged around camp, sullen as a sick bear, mixing very little with the men. The only one he seemed to talk with was Dusty.

Tin Pan, who now looked upon Anders as his savior, dogged his heels like a faithful hound, bringing him special little dishes and always keeping a pot of tea hot in the shack. Sluefoot seemed to know where he stood now. He surprised Anders, turning out to be an efficient foreman, getting work out of the men that would have pleased Colonel Mason himself.

Anders was glad to bury himself in the work, anything to keep his mind off Jamaica, exhausting himself so that he fell asleep immediately after dinner, too drugged for dreams. In three days they had almost finished the piers on both sides of the cañon. On the fourth morning Anders came from the engineer's shack, stopping just outside the door to look at the job. It was a frozen, diamond-bright morning. Distant snow surfaces made heliograph flashes in the early sun. Silver necklaces of ice dripped down the black rocks of the cañon.

Anders saw John Quill crossing from the barracks. He had probably not set traps for a year, but the stink of beaver medicine still clung to his greasy elk-hide leggings. A Green River knife in a brass-studded sheath hung around his neck on a rawhide thong, flapping against his belly as he walked. His long white hair, beaked nose, and rutted face made him look like an ancient Indian. He stopped before Anders, rubbing his elbows.

"Barton check in here last night?" he asked.

"Not to me."

Quill looked at the mountains. "We divided it

up. Hart and Joe Hide are patrollin' the upper section as far as the dam. Barton and me are on this lower end. He should have checked in last night and give me my turn."

"Why didn't you tell me last night?"

"He knows his country. His horse might've strayed or something. You got to give a little margin."

"Well, it may not be trouble," Anders said. "I should look at the flume anyway. Let's take a ride."

With the piers almost done there was nothing more they could do in camp till the wire came. Anders left Dusty in charge. Sluefoot had been straw boss on the flume from the beginning and Anders insisted that he go along to explain things, though the Pike was reluctant. They took a pack horse with enough grub for five days. Anders was still riding the paint from Grey's Livery. Quill rode a split-ear Indian pony with a mountain man's Crow saddle that was studded with brass and dripping with fringe and covered with bear claws and hawk bells and other fantastic decorations the trappers called foofaraw.

Twisting and turning, the flume led them upward and eastward, toward Lake Bigler, toward the backbone of the Sierras. The endless ranks of giant yellow pine seemed to march with them. The trees gave off the glitter and flash of a million knitting needles in the sun. There was snow everywhere, great drifts that were melting at the edges and giving a wet smell to the resin in the air. Quill rode ahead, off his nervous pony half the time, reading the sign Barton had left on his upward trip. He kept rubbing his elbows and he grimaced every time he dismounted.

"You got the ague?" Anders asked.

"Standin' to the hips in them mountain streams half my life," Quill said. "I'll be crippled up like an old squaw if I don't git back to Soda Springs."

"Soda Springs?"

A reverent light entered Quill's eyes. "Mountain man's heaven, Anders. I'll git enough money outen this to spend the rest o' my life jist sittin' in one o' them hot mud pools, drinkin' pop-skull till it comes outen my ears, waited on hand 'n' foot by the most sergiverous 'Rapahoe squaw you ever set eyes to."

Near noon they reached the spot where the flume crossed high above a creek on a confusing maze of trusses. Sluefoot said Garrett Mason had supervised the bridge.

"Something about combining Fink and Bollman," Sluefoot said. "What's that?"

"Trusses," Anders said. "Mason should have stuck with mining. He probably thought he'd get more strength from a compound truss. More likely they'll work against each other. Big wind, temperature change, high water . . . they'll pull each other apart."

Sluefoot grinned. "Anders, you know just too damn' much."

"A job for you, Sluefoot. When we get back to camp, send a crew up here. Take all those diagonals off. Strengthen your uprights with horizontal cross-ties and simple side buttresses. I'll draw you a picture."

By afternoon the wind was booming through the trees. It made the horses nervous and they kept shying at squirrels and woodpeckers. They were high and it was cold even in the sunlight. Anders had his Mackinaw on and his blanket wrapped around him and still he was shivering.

Near sundown they saw movement in a park high above them. They thought it was a deer at first, but they rode toward it anyway. Finally they saw that it was a buckskin drifting through a thin stand of maul oak and cropping peacefully at the flaky gray bark. Quill said it was Barton's horse.

The saddle had slipped around to hang below its belly, and the split reins were dragging the ground. Quill circled the horse, looking at the ground.

"Nothing here but horse tracks, and them a day old," he said.

They looked at each other. Anders started to speak, then closed his mouth. He didn't want to say what was on his mind.

They righted the saddle and cinched it up. With Sluefoot leading the horse, they followed its cold trail. It meandered back and forth till it finally led them back to the flume, a couple of miles higher than where they had left it.

It was demolished. Dynamite had apparently been planted at frequent intervals, digging deep holes in the earth, shattering the wooden aqueduct at each spot, littering the surrounding meadow with bits of the wreckage. Quill began to curse. They followed the course of the wreckage for two miles and he never stopped cursing. Finally they reached the end of it. The flume started again, running ahead of them over a ridge. They sat their horses on a slope, staring at the destruction on their back trail.

"How long will it take to repair?" Anders asked.

"Depends on how many men you send," Sluefoot said. "Count in felling new timber and splitting it out . . . a full crew could do the job in three or four days."

"How can you spare a full crew and git the bridge up, too?" Quill asked bitterly. "Don't you even care who did this, Anders?"

"What's your guess?" Anders asked.

"It's clear enough," Quill said. "Chileno and Leeper. They bore a grudge ag'in' you for givin' 'em the sack."

"Did they now?" Anders asked.

"Nothin' else makes sense," Sluefoot said.

"Doesn't it now?" Anders said. Sluefoot was

frowning curiously at him. Anders made an angry motion with one hand. "We still haven't found Barton."

They went on following the tracks. There was snow drifted across the rocky meadows and up against the plank sides of the flume. In the shelter of timber, where the shade would keep the sun from melting it, a deep imprint left its brand in the snowbank. It was the size and shape of a man's body, with the arms and legs outflung. Some of the outline at the top had been obliterated by the dragging track that led out of the snowbank.

"Looks like his horse pitched him off and he crawled out of the drift," Sluefoot offered.

"Somethin' more than the horse pitched him," Quill said.

"What?"

Quill was looking at the dark stain in the snow about where the man's head would have been. "You don't get a nosebleed fallin' in a snowbank," Quill said.

Barton had left a plain trail. Sometimes walking, sometimes dragging himself along, he had moved higher into the mountains. The trail veered crazily across snow-mantled meadows, looped through stands of timber. Night came, bitter and cold. Quill finally halted his pony. He was bent over with his arthritis, hugging himself and shivering and rubbing his elbows.

"That's about it. I can't see no tracks in this

168

dark. My misery won't let me go on in this cold."

"We can't wait till morning," Anders said. "If Barton was wounded, he won't last much longer in this. We'll light a torch."

He found some pine knots and they followed the tracks by their flaring torchlight. Quill's arthritis was getting worse all the time. He couldn't straighten in the saddle, and though he would not complain, Anders could see the pain in his eyes.

They reached a fire forest. Lightning had perhaps started the blaze and the holocaust had swept for miles through the lodgepoles. Most of the great charred matchsticks still stood, the ashen litter of the fire buried beneath deep snowdrifts in their bases. The trail led directly into the ghostly tree cemetery.

The moon began to rise. For a hundred yards Quill could still find Barton's trail. The drifts deepened. It had apparently snowed here after Barton had passed through, and had covered all sign of the man.

They stopped the horses and the shivering animals stood knee-deep in the drift. The moon was high enough now so that there was no more need of the torch. Anders dropped it and the pine knot sputtered and went out. Some of the charred trees that towered over the men had broken off at the tops. But the lodgepoles were ranked so closely that the fallen had been caught in the arms of their brothers. They surrounded the men in a grotesque etching of death, a horde of ashen skeletons traced blackly against the pale glare of moonlit snow.

"I can't go no farther," Quill said. He was bent forward till his chest rested against the brass-studded pommel of his saddle. "This misery's laid aholt on me too strong, boys. I can't go on."

Anders took his reins and led the skittish Indian pony through the dead, crackling timber till they reached a park. He told Sluefoot to gather some dead boughs. Anders kicked snow away till he reached solid ground. He made a bed of the boughs. He got Quill off his pony and put the man's horse blanket on the boughs. He set Quill on that and wrapped his own blanket around the crippled man. He and Sluefoot went out for more wood, finding enough that was only partially charred. They built a fire as near Quill as they could. Anders made some coffee and put the whole pot beside Quill. He loaded the trapper's rifle and put it at hand, unsheathed his Green River knife and put it in his lap.

"There's meat and hardtack in the grab sack," Anders said. "You can last a couple of days, can't you?"

Quill nodded. "Long's the grub holds out."

"If you mean you're goin' now, you'll go alone," Sluefoot said.

Anders took out his Walker and cocked it. "I'm

170

too cold to argue, Sluefoot. Get on your horse."
The Pike took out his Henry Clay. The plug was cased so heavily that when he bit off a chew it released a smell of licorice and molasses that hung like syrup in the brittle air. Sluefoot looked at the big Colt in Anders's hand. Perhaps he was remembering Leeper. He put his chewing tobacco back in his shirt pocket and mounted his horse.

Several times Quill had commented that Barton was moving uphill all the time, as though he was running from something. It was all Anders had to go on. The slant of the slope steepened. Soon the horses were belly-deep in snow, floundering and wheezing. The trees were so close that the animals could hardly get through them. They were constantly ramming the trunks, squealing as bark and hide came off together. It made the brittle trees shake. It started a ghostly rattling among the fallen limbs trapped in the charred maze of branches above the men. Sluefoot tried to stop three or four times, and Anders had to force him on with the gun. When they finally reached timberline, the horses were shuddering and shiny with sweat.

Anders pushed into the open. It was below freezing. His joints ached and all feeling was gone from his face. He spurred his horse higher, wanting to get a view from the ridge. He was a hundred feet from timberline when there was an ear-splitting crack. The echoes rolled down through the burn in peals of thunder. The paint reared and pitched Anders.

The snow cushioned his fall and he came up gasping. There was another crack, another. He recognized them as gunshots now. He saw bark chipped from a tree three feet away. A ricochet screamed weirdly. Sluefoot had already reined his horse back into the timber and was down in the snow, pulling his rifle from its scabbard.

"It looks like he's up in those rocks!" Anders shouted. "Cover me. I'll try to get above him."

The ridge above timberline was a maze of granite outcroppings. Snow lay deep in the hollows and gullies between each naked spur of rock. Anders floundered laterally through the shelter of the blackened trees till he reached some cap rock that ran down into the timber. It gave him the cover to move out of the lodgepoles. There was another shot and chipped rock spat at him from six feet away. He waited for Sluefoot's answering shot. It did not come.

Someone was shouting now. Anders couldn't make out the words. It had a weird cadence, like an Indian chant, or a crazy song. It grew louder as he crawled upward. He had already worked too hard in the high altitude. He was gasping for breath. The air was thin and acrid and tasted like smoke. It burned his throat and hurt his lungs. His ribs ached and his vision was beginning to jump.

But he would not stop. He had the sense of coming to grips with something at last. All the unanswered questions . . . Cousin Jack's hostility . . . the freighter on the Mountain House Grade . . . the landslide that had almost buried him at Satan's Keyhole.

The shouting had stopped. He checked himself, crouched on his hands and knees behind the broken ledges of granite. How long ago had it stopped? There was a roaring in his head. He was shaking and sick with exhaustion. He had his gun out and the grips were slimy with his sweat.

He started to move again. He heard a rattling on his flank, a little behind. He wheeled. Like some monster out of the earth a man towered against the moon. He was only three feet away, on top of the rocks. It was Barton and he had a Dragoon Colt pointed at Anders's face.

In automatic reflex Anders jerked his gun up. But his hand was so numb he couldn't make his finger pull the trigger. It didn't matter. He couldn't have fired before Barton. The Dragoon's hammer snapped. If there had been a load in the chamber, it would have blown Anders's head off.

Barton shouted in frustration and flung the empty gun at Anders. Anders jerked aside and it struck his shoulder. Barton came down on Anders with all his clawing weight.

They struck the ground with Barton on top.

Snarling and cursing, the man fought to maim Anders, to kill him.

Anders still held his gun. He finally got his arm free and struck Barton across the side of the head. The man went limp. Anders crawled out from under him and sprawled flat. The violence at such an altitude had left him completely spent. He couldn't get enough air. His ribs ached intolerably with every breath. He couldn't even move when Sluefoot came up.

"He's out of his head," he gasped. "He's crazy."

Finally he was able to sit up. He looked at the front of Barton's shirt. It had been soaked with blood. The blood was dried now. It had frozen and matted and had stuck the shirt to the man's body. Barton moaned feebly, his eyes fluttered. He looked blankly at Anders. He flailed the ground with one arm and started to rise, his face loose and wild again. But the fight had finished him. He made a moaning sound and sank back.

"Barton," Anders said. "Who shot you? It's Anders, Barton. Who wrecked the flume and shot you?"

Barton's eyes turned blank and childish. He smiled weirdly. "Sam," he said, "when did you shave off your beard?"

X

They went back to the clearing where they had left Quill. Barton was still delirious, but too weak to fight any more. When they got his shirt off, they saw how bad the wound was, angling up through his ribs from front to back. Quill told them how to make a primitive poultice of lard and gunpowder. They took watches to keep a fire going and tend the sick man through the night.

Only the immense animal vitality of these mountain men had kept Barton alive. It was dangerous to move him, but they all agreed that it would be more dangerous to try to keep him alive here, without shelter, without a doctor.

The day's warmth eased Quill's misery a little and he was able to move around. They made an Indian travois for a litter—a pair of poles forked together over the rump of Barton's horse, their butt ends dragging the ground. It was bumpy and they had to go slow but it was easier on the man than putting him in the saddle.

Barton was out of his head all the time. Anders tried to question him again but he could get nothing coherent out of the man. Barton kept calling him Sam. Quill said Sam was Barton's brother, who had been killed by the Utes in New Mexico years ago.

They reached the Keyhole on the third day after leaving the burn. The whole crew came from the cabins and cook fires to meet them. As Anders dismounted, he saw Eddie Norris among them.

Anders told them what had happened. Then, as the men lifted Barton out of the travois, Anders turned to Norris.

"At least it isn't all bad news, Eddie. How soon will the wire be along?"

Norris looked at his shoes, scuffing them in the dirt. "There isn't any wire, Glenn."

"What?"

Norris fingered his face nervously. "The harbor master couldn't tell me much. There was some freight due on the wire. A man paid it and hauled the wire away."

"That doesn't make sense, Eddie. It was junk. It was with a lot of other junk that had been rotting on the beach for months. What could they use it for?"

"The harbor master mentioned mine cables."

"It would have to be spun. They don't have the machines for that out here. This man who took it . . ."

"The harbor master said his name was Corey, from Sacramento Shippers. I checked at Sacramento on my way back. The shipping company didn't know anything about it. . . ."

Anders wasn't even listening. *Corey.* It was the last thing he had really heard Eddie say. *Kettle*

Corey. And the big Sacramento Shippers freight wagon on the Mountain House Grade just outside Downieville, forcing them to take the Concord coach apart. Anders looked toward Barton. He had felt so close up there, so near the answer. He almost went after the wounded man. But he knew it was hopeless. Barton would only call him Sam and say he should have left his beard on.

Anders bowed his head. Exhaustion swept over him like an overpowering weight. His joints ached and there was a sickly sweet taste in his mouth. He wanted to go somewhere, sit down, lie down, close his eyes, close his mind to all this.

The men waited, watching him. He knew he should give them some definite assurance. There were still decisions to make, orders to give. But he could think of nothing to tell them. What was the use of sending a crew to repair the flume if they couldn't put up the bridge? They seemed to sense his uncertainty. They stirred restlessly, looking at each other. He was up against a blank wall, and he knew it and they knew it.

For some reason it made him think of Jamaica. He was filled with the same sense of frustration, of inadequacy that he always felt with her. Was it going to be Mast Hope again? Was it going to be Chicago? Was it going to be every failure he had ever known with her, all over again?

"Could we do it with ropes?" Norris asked.

"What?"

"The bridge. Mister Mason said that down in Peru the Indians make suspension bridges of rope. They last for centuries."

"And only a few men crossing at a time. Do you realize the volume of water we'll be carrying, Eddie? The oscillation you'll get? The rope would be chewed to bits."

Norris did not answer. There was a look of confusion in his eyes, almost disillusionment. Anders turned away from it and went to the engineer's shack.

He knew they had to give Barton a rest before they moved him on down to Hangtown. Anders was so exhausted that he slept the rest of that day and the whole night through. The next morning they put Barton back in his travois. The man was still delirious and recognized none of them. Anders took Norris and Quill with him.

Near evening the trail crossed a wagon road. Norris told Anders the road led to the Golden Monte. It was only a mile out of their way. Anders knew it would be easier on Barton if they could get him into a wagon. Quill stayed with the wounded man at the crossing while Anders and Norris rode to the mine.

They were passing through some scrubby maul oak when Anders's paint began to shy and fight the bit. Anders had the shadowy impression of a rider in the timber on their flank. He was still jumpy from the hunt for Barton. He pulled his gun, fighting the nervous horse, and called to the man.

"All right! Come on out!"

There was the crackle of underbrush as the rider pushed his big calico mule into the open. Anders could not hide his surprise. The man was Chinese.

"Charlie," Anders said.

Hangtown Charlie grinned blandly. He wore his conical bamboo hat and his matted buffalo coat and a pair of elk-hide leggings that some trapper must have left on the dump heap.

"You go to mine, Mistuh Anduhs?" he asked.

"That's right. What are you doing here, Charlie?"

The Chinese slapped his saddlebags. "Chollie takee gin to the minuhs. Chollie go with you?"

Anders hesitated, wondering why he was so suspicious. Norris said: "What's the harm, Glenn? You're liable to find Charlie anywhere up here."

Anders put his gun away and nodded at Charlie. A few hundred yards on they came to a creek, a trickle of icy water between banks of dirty ice. On either side ran the familiar network of flumes and sluice boxes, the rusting hydraulic monitors, the crumbling cliffs that had been cut away by the relentless streams of water. It all had the forlorn, deserted air of a ghost town.

The horse shied again, so sharply that Anders was almost pitched. This time he did not have time to get his gun out. A pair of men had stepped from the maze of flumes beside the road. They both wore cast-off Army greatcoats and fur hats. One of them carried an old Springfield with a Maynard tape primer rolled in its magazine. "I thought you was going to light a shuck," he said to Charlie.

"Chollie with Mistuh Anduhs."

Anders told them what he wanted. The man scowled at him, considering it. Finally he said: "That Chink doesn't go with you. We don't want no Chinks in the diggings."

"Chollie give you flee bottle of ginnee."

The man lifted his Springfield. "If you don't git, I'm a-goin' to blow you and your gin clear back to Hangtown."

Charlie looked pleadingly at Anders. Anders said nothing. Charlie sighed, straightened his bamboo hat, and turned the mule back down the road. One of the guards took Anders and Norris up the road. There was a collection of weather-blackened log buildings near the mouth of an adit. The guard got the foreman from one of the cabins, a big sullen man named Yuba. He said he could give them a buckboard, but no team. Anders said they'd try their saddlers in harness. The buckboard was near the mouth of the adit. While they were hitching up, Anders heard a steam engine going inside the tunnel.

He glanced at Norris, then walked to the mouth

of the adit. Inside he could see a miner standing by the windlass. His lantern cast a smoky glow over the cable coiled on the winch.

The mine cage came up and the steam engine stopped. Three sweating, grimy miners stepped off the platform. Anders saw Yuba coming from the buildings.

"I thought you wanted a wagon," the foreman said.

"Are you working the mine this early?" Anders said.

"A cave-in blocked the main adit. We're trying to get it cleared."

"How far down?"

"At the eighteen hundred-foot-level. Listen, mister . . ."

"That cable. It looks machine-spun."

"None better. Charcoal wire, forty tons to the square inch."

Anders looked at Eddie Norris. The boy was smiling excitedly. A pulse began to thump in Anders's temple. Eighteen hundred feet of machine-spun cable! Anders told Yuba what he wanted. Yuba said he didn't have authorization to give Anders any cable. "And if you don't git out of here in five minutes with that wagon, mister, you can damn' well go without it," he added.

They could move faster with Barton in the wagon. They reached Hangtown after nightfall.

They found a doctor to treat the wound, and then bedded him down in a cabin just outside town that the four trappers had used earlier in the year. Leaving Quill with Barton, Anders and Norris went to the Riley boarding house. Mrs. Riley said that the King's Players were in town and Mason had felt strong enough for Opal to take him to see the play at Grey's Livery.

They had taken down the rail stalls in Grey's barn and had pegged together some puncheon benches for the miners to sit on. They had improvised some Phoebe lamps by filling a dozen iron kettles with sand, sinking a wick in it, and soaking the sand with lard. The blackened kettles hung from the rafters and the heated sand filled the big barn with the smell of rancid fat. The weird saffron light seemed to pluck the mob of faces from the shadows, turning them to a sea of bearded, gibbous moons. The raised section at the rear of the barn that Grey had been using for a loft was cleared of feed and hay to give the players their stage. It was dressed with a crude assortment of furniture. Parker Innes, in a purple frock coat and a green beaver hat, was filling the windy building with his booming voice.

"Your extravagance will ruin me, Missus Tiffany."

"And your stinginess will ruin me, Mister Tiffany. . . ."

It was Jamaica, in a white satin gown, the

emerald tiara Anders had given her in New Orleans burning like a weird green fire in the bizarre light. It made him forget the Masons. He had to stop and watch. In the first moment he was conscious of her jerky, marionette's movement as she crossed the stage, her broad gestures, the way she contorted her face into the expression he knew so well, always the same expression, whether she was portraying comedy or tragedy, passion or humor, anguish or remorse. Why the devil did she have to "act" when she was on the stage? Her movements were so graceful when she was not conscious of an audience. He had seen the natural expressions on her face, when she was asleep or relaxed or off guard. There was nothing more beautiful.

Then he lost the sense of the synthetic. She cast her spell over him, as she did over the crowd of avid miners. He was one of them. They hadn't seen a woman like this in years. Maybe some of them had never seen a woman like this. They spent their life digging earth out of some black hole a thousand feet deep or standing to their knees with a pick and pan in some icy river. For months all they knew of womanhood were the girls on some red-light line, a pockmarked half-breed, or a fourteen-year-old slave girl from the Chinese cribs. Jamaica could have stood on the stage without saying a word and they would stay all night to watch.

". . . it is totally and toot-a-fate impossible to convince you of the necessity of keeping up appearances . . . merely because I required a paltry fifty dollars to purchase a new style of headdress, a bijou of an article just introduced in France . . ." Parker Innes put one hand to his lapel and struck a pose. "Time was, Missus Tiffany, when you manufactured your own French headdresses. . . ."

Anders finally saw Garrett Mason sitting on Grey's own rickety chair, wrapped to the eyes in a greatcoat and heavy muffler. Opal was with him. She had on the same porkpie hat and fur coat she had worn when he first met her at Downieville. Her father was intent on the play, but she saw Anders and moved out to meet him.

"We thought you'd be coming back," she said.

"Your father must be better," he said.

"The doctor let him out of bed. He was so worried about losing the wire . . . I thought the play might take his mind off it."

"Glenn has an idea," Eddie Norris said.

Opal didn't even look at him. She reached out and caught Anders's hand. "I knew you'd come up with something."

"Maybe your father's already thought of it. The cable at the Golden Monte."

She held his hand a moment longer, then let it go. He saw the darkness in her blue eyes. "Well," she said, "we can try."

He frowned. "What's the matter?"

"Well . . . you'd better tell Dad."

Anders went to Mason. The old engineer showed the same lack of enthusiasm. He doubted if the Golden Monte would give up the wire. Anders asked where Victor Castine was.

"He's been a stage-door Johnny ever since the players opened," Mason said.

Anders hesitated. He knew he would have to see Jamaica. It had been his main reason for staying, for taking the job. To see her as often as possible, to get her back somehow . . . "I'll see Castine," he said.

Mason started to rise, too, but Opal caught his arm. "You stay here. It's too cold out there for you."

Behind the barn was an outbuilding housing a tack room and bunkhouse. The players were using the side door of the barn for their exits and entrances. Just outside stood the inevitable gawking group of men, shivering in the cold. A quarreling wardrobe mistress was trying to keep them from blocking the door. Victor Castine stood aside, his greatcoat collar turned up, holding a cloak for Jamaica. He was watching her through the open door, and did not even seem aware of Anders. The look on his face was all too familiar to the engineer.

"Castine," Anders said.

The man started slightly. The glazed look

left his eyes and he focused them with some effort on Anders. "Ah . . . Anders . . . isn't she magnificent? I think this is her best rôle. Why does she waste such talent on this backwater? She should be touring Europe. I told her . . ."

"Castine, what's the biggest part of your operation?"

"What?"

"The Golden Monte. What percent of it is quartz mining?"

Castine looked at him narrowly. "Who have you been talking to?"

"Nobody. We went to the mine. It didn't look like you'd taken anything out of that hole for months."

"Well, that cave-in . . . played hob with our operation. When we get it cleared away . . ."

"Even then, what percentage will it be?"

"Well . . . ah . . . I'd say twenty-five or thirty. . . ."

He broke off. He was still looking beyond Anders, through the door. Anders heard Jamaica's voice.

". . . to lose at once a title and a beau."

There was a pause, and then the cast came hurrying through the door. The applause was deafening. The miners roared and stamped and Anders could hear the clatter of money and gold thrown on the stage. Jamaica was flushed, her eyes glittering. Castine stepped forward with the cloak, but Jamaica turned back toward the door, leaving him with the cloak held in mid-air. She saw Anders and her mouth opened in a delightful, calculated little expression of pleased surprise.

"Ah, Glenn, darling . . ."

"Jamaica," he said, "I've got to see you."

"Later, *ma foi*, later. . . ."

Parker Innes caught her hand, pulling her through the door for the curtain calls. Castine was still holding the cloak up. He smiled sheepishly, lowering it. Anders felt just as foolish. The miners were grinning at him and he felt his cheeks go hot. They took a half dozen curtain calls before Jamaica would finally stay outside, accepting the cloak. She was the center of attention, chattering breathlessly.

"Lewis *cheri*, you simply must quit stepping all over my lines . . . pull the collar down, Victor . . . careful, *sacre bleu*, the hair . . . Parker, if you don't let me wait for that laugh, I'll cross right in front of you. . . ." She started toward the dressing room, surrounded by her court. As if in afterthought she halted a moment, sending a brilliant smile over her shoulder. "Glenn, Victor is giving a little party for us at the hotel. Won't you come?"

The memories came at him in one overwhelming picture—the glittering, laughing, vivid people, a language he did not understand, drinking too much, talking too much, a foreigner in their nightmare world, 3:00 in the morning, the bursts of garish laughter jarring his head, the loose faces swimming at him through a smoke-filled room. . . . "I'm sorry," he said. "I just got in from the job. I'm hardly dressed."

She laughed, sending a knowing glance at Castine. "You'll have to excuse him, Victor. He never really felt at home with show people."

Anders flushed. "On second thought," he said grimly, "I think I'll accept the invitation."

XI

The hotel suite was blue with smoke and jammed with people. Most of the leading townsmen were in the crowd, including Garrett Mason and his daughter. Mason had brought Cousin Jack. Anders saw the Cornishman by a window, glancing out now and then as though seeking escape. He held a drink untouched in one hand, a big, awkward, thoroughly miserable man, as out of place as a surly bear in a cage of chattering monkeys.

Garrett Mason was sneaking a drink with Parker Innes. Opal had been captured by the younger men. Eddie Norris stood on the outside of the group, pulling uncomfortably at his collar and staring resentfully around the room. Anders cut two supers and offered one to the young man.

188

"You'll get used to it, Eddie. When you get your craw full, just ask one of them to step out in the hall."

The boy grinned gratefully and accepted the cigar. Anders lit them both. He drew deep, glancing at another group of men. Victor Castine was among them, and through their bobbing, nodding, fawning heads he could catch glimpses of Jamaica's flashing eyes and Jamaica's red lips and Jamaica's glittering jewelry. She was laughing too much and she was talking in three languages and she gestured with every word and it always seemed to be the same gesture. He had the violent urge to drag her out of the room and take her by the shoulders and shake her like a little girl till there wasn't an affectation left in her. He emitted cigar smoke in a pungent gust.

In a corner he saw Laurette Castine huddled in a chair by the soapstone stove, fussing to pull her opera cloak more protectively around her shoulders. Dr. Magwell Reed hovered at her elbow, but she seemed oblivious to what he was saying. She was watching her husband and Jamaica. Anders could read her expression clearly, for it came from an emotion that was very familiar to him. Her face was pale and pinched and vicious with jealousy.

"If you know Buchanan at all," Dr. Reed was saying, "you know that he went beyond Psychometry and Sarcognomy and explained anthropology through its mathematical key, Pathognomy. The pathognomic lines of the organs which would interfere, clash, and produce antagonism when two heads faced each other, would run parallel, coincide and produce sympathy when they faced in the same direction."

"That sounds like a universal principle," Anders said. "If everybody faced in the same direction all the time, it would probably do away with wars, pestilence, green sickness, and the Whig tariff."

The doctor glared at Anders. Laurette Castine was still looking at her husband. "Doctor," she said, "I feel my vapors gathering. You promised me some of that Peruvian bark."

"In my room, madam, in my room. I have been at the mortar and pestle all day. It will take me but a moment."

Dr. Reed swept out of the room. Without looking at Anders, Laurette nodded her head at the men around Jamaica. "I should think you would do something about that."

"I might say the same about you."

The woman sniffed. "I indulge him."

"By inviting actresses to be your companion?"

"If it's going to go on, isn't it better to have it going on under my eye? It's actually harmless. Victor is like a little boy. He always comes back."

"When you pull the purse strings," he said. She glanced at him narrowly. He studied the glowing end of his cigar. "Perhaps I've been talking to the wrong one. Victor tells me your quartz mining accounts form only twenty-five percent of the Golden Monte's yield."

"Something like that."

"So if Mason doesn't get this water to you, three-fourths of your operation will be cut off."

"Obviously."

"Wouldn't it be better to sacrifice the one-fourth you have now for the three-fourths you'd get back with the water?"

"What are you getting at?"

"You must know that we couldn't get the cable in Frisco. The cable you have at the Golden Monte could do the job."

She sneezed, pulling her cloak up. "Would you see if that window is open?"

"It's closed tight, Missus Castine. Don't try to put me off. You're too smart a woman to cut your own throat. It's simple arithmetic. Give up the cable and you triple the capacity you'd get if you keep it."

"We couldn't make such a decision. The board would have to be convened, a vote taken, a report to the stockholders . . ."

"As chairman of the board, Victor certainly has emergency powers. If you don't act now, you'll lose your whole hydraulic operation."

She shook her head. "Victor could not authorize any such move. It would involve much more than simply giving you the cable. It would mean shutting down completely. You can't imagine the ramifications, the effect on the stock, the reverberations in the East."

"Anything like the earthquake when you have to report a seventy-five percent cutback?"

"It's out of our hands, Mister Anders. We simply cannot give you the cable."

Dr. Magwell Reed pushed his way through the crowd, carrying an armful of bottles. The troupe's comic grabbed Anders's arm. He was a drunken little cherub in a bowler and a checkered weskit.

"Tell me, mister, when are soldiers not soldiers?"

"When they're mustered," Anders said.

The comic gaped. "You must have seen me in Frisco."

"I've seen you in Frisco, New Orleans, New York. . . ."

"I wasn't in New York."

"I've even seen you in my nightmares."

The second lead pushed his way into the conversation. "Did I hear you mention New York? Did you see Anna Mowatte do her play there?"

"Not at the time," Anders said.

"Do you think Mister Tiffany is really patterned after Missus Mowatte's own husband?"

"I didn't know her husband."

"But there must be some connection. That business with Davenport, touring all of Europe . . ."

"He *was* her leading man," Anders said.

"Ah . . . *touché!*"

"By all means *touché!*"

Parker Innes appeared from somewhere, carrying a half empty glass and making loose shapes with his mouth. He pulled Anders away, throwing an arm over his shoulder.

"You'll have to pardon my brusqueness at Grass Valley, Anders. If I'd known you were Jamaica's husband . . ."

"Never mind. It happens all the time."

Parker Innes nodded. "You're in a foreign land, aren't you?"

"Hardly," Anders said. "After all, I spent several years in New York."

"Don't bother. I can see it on your face." Innes hiccupped. "Well, we're brothers under the skin, Anders. Sometimes I feel like a lost sheep m'self. D' y'know that? Forty years in the theater, and a lost sheep. There are some genuine people in this strange land, Anders, and when you're in the presence o' one it's no more a dream. Junius Brutus Booth! When I first met him, 'twas after *Richard the Third*, in New York. I wanted to kneel at his feet, Anders. Literally. As a man would kneel before God. He was crazy and he was drunk but there was a fire blazing up in him and it lighted up a dark world for a minute."

"I saw him."

Innes squinted at him. The drunken looseness was gone momentarily from the older man's face.

"Of course y'did. And you know what I'm talkin' about. There are some great ones in your world, too, aren't there?"

"A Colonel Mason," Anders said.

"And some fakes. Y'know the fakes when you see them, just as y'know the real articles. Y'know something, Anders? Your wife's a fake."

"Innes . . ."

"You know I'm right." The man laughed, hanging to him heavily. "She doesn't belong in this world, does she?"

"I don't know . . . acting . . . I know so little about the theater. . . ."

"Zounds! What must one know?" Innes's voice was growing louder and people in the room were beginning to turn. "Either the spark is there or it isn't. The holy light. If it's there, a child can see it. Get her out, Anders. Jamaica doesn't belong. She knows she doesn't belong. There are other worlds, Anders. A thousand of them. She could be a queen in any of them. I'm a traitor, Anders. I've betrayed myself, her, the theater itself. The miners would pay a fortune just to look at her. They didn't care if she could act or not. Who am I to leave gold lying in the street? I put her on the boards. I made her my leading lady. I'm living a lie, Anders, and I'm ashamed of myself. . . ."

He trailed off, looking beyond Anders. His mouth made loose shapes and a tremor ran through his furred jowls. Anders realized that most of the talk in the room had stopped. He turned to see everyone staring at Innes. And not ten feet away stood Jamaica, her face crimson.

"You drunken old fool," she said. She walked toward Innes and her voice rang shrilly through the room, stopping whoever was still talking. "You malicious, drunken, lying old fool!"

She slapped Innes. It jarred his head and left the white imprint of her fingers against his flushed cheek. Jamaica whirled and plunged blindly through the crowd into the bedroom, slamming the door behind her.

Anders crossed after her, trying to open the door. But she had turned the key. He had followed her on an angry impulse and now he was sorry. He felt foolish and inept, standing futilely at the door. Everybody seemed to be looking at him. He could hear Jamaica's muffled sobs from within the room. There was something pathetic about it. He could not be angry with her any longer. He could only feel sorry for her.

Parker Innes made a broad gesture, and his voice boomed through the room. "I didn't think she had it in her. Egad, the scene was so good, we'll have to write it into *Nick o' the Woods*."

A wave of embarrassed laughter ran through the crowd. Self-consciously they tried to start their conversations again. Innes looked at Anders, tried to smile, and headed for the liquor.

Anders moved away from the door. He saw the comic heading toward him and avoided the man. He became aware of Cousin Jack, still by the window, looking intently at something in the street. The big man frowned; his lips moved soundlessly. He put his drink down, without becoming aware of Anders, and headed for the door.

Curiosity prompted Anders to walk to the window. For a moment, dark outside and light inside, it was like trying to look through a mirror. Then the torches on the hotel's overhang outside seemed to bloom through the opaque glass. They cast vague yellow light across the passing shapes of men and the big freight wagon halted at the curb. A man stood by the wagon, looking up at the window. He had a powder-keg shape to his huge torso and all he wore in the bitterly cold night was a wool shirt with the sleeves rolled above the elbows. As Anders watched, he took an ivory snuffbox from his pocket, rolled snuff into a ball, and tucked it beneath his upper lip. He moved away from the freight wagon. Anders could see the sign on its side: Sacramento Shippers.

XII

Anders pushed through the theater crowd, spilling someone's drink, and reached the door. Cousin Jack was not in the hall or on the stairs. Anders hurried through the lobby. As he stepped outside, he saw Cousin Jack and Kettle Corey standing by the freight wagon, arguing heatedly. They turned without seeing Anders and started up the street, still arguing.

Anders followed, jostled by the crowds. Even at this hour the men were working their coyote holes in the middle of Main. Some of them were below street level, throwing dirt out of the holes for others to pan by the light of lanterns or pine torches. Anders threaded his way through the weird traps, watching the two men ahead so intently that he almost pitched head foremost into one of the makeshift mines.

The crowd hid the Cornishman and the teamster. Anders hurried to get closer. When he saw them again, they had reached the huge oak and were parting. Cousin Jack said something to Kettle, shook his fist in the man's face, and headed toward Grey's Livery. Kettle looked after him, took a pinch of snuff, and turned down toward the creek.

Anders halted under the hang tree, suspicion

and curiosity a pressure inside him, undecided about which man to follow. Finally he went after Kettle.

The teamster led him through a motley collection of tents and outbuildings. For a moment Anders thought he was heading for the red-light line. There was a row of squalid shacks, the music of a banjo, and the shrill laughter of a drunken woman. Over some of the doors lanterns had been hung, illuminating the names painted on puncheon boards: Suzie, Spanish Lou, Grizzly Gertie, Laura . . .

But Kettle passed the red-light line, heading up the frozen bank of Hangtown Creek. Ahead was the dump heap of the town and a huddle of flimsy shacks built of cast-off lumber and flattened tin cans and other refuse. The faint smell of incense penetrated even the reek of the garbage heaps, and Anders knew where he was.

The lure of gold that had drawn men from every corner of the world had not missed the Orient. The first Chinese to reach California had arrived with a shipload of Kanakas from the Sandwich Islands. Since then they had come to the golden shore in an ever-growing tide. San Francisco's Chinatown was already famous, and almost every gold camp had its counterpart in miniature.

But only one of the shacks seemed occupied. The yellow square of its single window shone forlornly in the abandoned camp. Doors gaped open in the other hovels. Charred walls had fallen, a wind rattled mournfully at the loose tin shingles. Anders remembered what Dusty had said about Chinese Moving Day, and the cook at Satan's Keyhole with his tongue cut out. . . .

Kettle stopped before the occupied shack, shaking the whole structure with his knock. Without waiting for an answer, he pushed open the door and went inside. There was a parrot-like chatter of Chinese, then Kettle's rough voice. The talk dropped to an unintelligible murmur.

Anders stood in the darkness outside, uncertain now. Suddenly somebody shouted from within the house. There was a crash of broken furniture and the whole structure shook. A woman screamed, and then began talking Chinese in a wild, shrill voice.

Anders started for the door, hand on his gun. The door was flung open and a dim shape ran by him—the woman, still wailing. Inside, by the weird light of a broken lantern, Anders could see Kettle struggling with a Chinese.

"There's wire up there, Charlie, there's a hundred places with wire. You're a-goin' t' tell me iffen I have to bust it outta you bone by bone . . . !"

Anders lunged through the door, pulling his gun, calling sharply: "Corey!"

The teamster glanced aside, still holding the Chinese. When he saw Anders, he let out a roaring curse and swung the man around, flinging him like an empty sack. Anders couldn't fire without hitting the Chinese. The man went into him violently, knocking the gun from his hand and carrying them both back against the wall. Kettle was already running out the door.

Anders pushed the Chinese away and dived for the teamster. His shoulder caught Kettle, spinning him aside, and they both went headlong out the door. Anders rolled and came up. He saw the huge man in front of him, rising, too. He didn't have time to block the blow.

It jarred the world. He fell back against the house, stunned, everything spinning. His head was roaring. He made pawing motions, trying to rise, trying to see. He was aware of someone crouched a few feet away, whining at him in Chinese.

"Sun more see, Amelica, sun more see. . . ."

It was the girl who had run past Anders. She was really little more than a child, barefoot and dressed in a flimsy rag. She couldn't have been more than twelve or thirteen. She had the hopeless, sunken, diseased face of a very old woman.

Anders got to his feet, holding his aching jaw. He knew that Kettle was lost to him, gone in the night. He saw Hangtown Charlie standing in the doorway. The ex-conductor wore an embroidered coat of black and white silk that hung to his knees. His queue pulled his hair like a wet black skullcap against his head, and his smooth face shimmered like wet copper in the dim light. He smiled blandly at Anders.

"Ah, Missuh Anduhs, you wantee more ginee?"

"You can drop the laundryman act, Charlie. I know you can talk English better than I can."

"Missuh Anduhs, a Chinese has as much chance of achievin' the Amelican L as the plove'bial camel has of passin' through the eye of the needle."

"You've got the American R all right. I heard you cussing when you bumped your head under that California stage. And you didn't learn all those words from any parrot."

"Pallot?"

"It's no use, Charlie. What was Kettle Corey doing here?"

"Ah, yes, Kettle Corey." Charlie crossed his arms over his belly, put his hands in his sleeves, and bowed his head. "I give you poor thanks for saving my inconsequential life."

The flawless English made Anders lift his brows. "I thought so," he said.

"Do you know what a mandarin is, Mister Anders?"

"Sort of like royalty in your country, isn't it?"

"I had a tutor from Oxford, and my fingernails were eight inches long."

Anders looked at the miserable shack. "Quite a comedown."

"As the sun sets at night, so it must inevitably rise again in the morning. Perhaps you will honor my house?"

He backed into the room. Anders looked at the girl. She went in and kneeled silently in a corner. He followed. There was the smell of gin and rice and pork in the room. Some red paper covered with Chinese ideographs had been pasted on one wall in a pathetic effort to cover the chinks. The girl's hopeless black eyes were fixed dully on Anders. It disturbed him. He retrieved his gun and holstered it.

"What's going on, Charlie?" Anders asked. "What's back of all this? Who's trying to stop Mason?"

"The Sphinx's questions have no answer, Mister Anders."

"I think mine have. There's an ugly thought in my head, Charlie. You keep popping up. You were on the stage when Kettle first showed up outside Downieville. Kettle took that wire off the beach at Frisco. And now Kettle comes to you and it's about wire. Maybe you're behind it, Charlie. Or maybe it's the Six Companies. Are they trying to stop Mason from getting the bridge through?"

"What would they gain by that?"

"I don't know. Maybe revenge. You've been treated like hell in this country."

Charlie's smile made oblique slits of his eyes.

Anders could not tell if his round, fat moon of a face looked very comical or very serious. The man made a gesture with one hand and the girl crept across the floor to place a rusty kettle on a brazier in the corner. Charlie seated himself on a bamboo mat, ceremoniously arranging a pair of tea cups before him.

"The Six Companies have been accused of many fantastic things, Mister Anders. They are nothing more than merchant associations organized in San Francisco for the protection and guidance of the Chinese."

"And they own you like slaves," Anders said. "Where does all the money go that you pay in?"

"When we die, it returns our bones to the Flowery Kingdom."

"It doesn't take that much to get you back to China. The Six Companies own a million dollars' worth of real estate in Frisco alone, Charlie. What else do they own? Sacramento Shippers?"

The water began to boil. The girl sprinkled some tea into the cups and poured them full. She crept back to her corner. Charlie waved his hand at the mat in front of him. Anders hesitated, angry, confused, balked by the bland enigma of the Orient. He finally sat down, hitching his gun around to lie in his lap. Charlie watched the tea leaves settle in the darkening water.

"You were not here in the first years," Charlie said. "During 'Forty-Nine, when it was new to everybody, and my people were not so many, we were allowed to stake claims like everybody else. But soon we grew too numerous. There are over twenty five thousand of us here now. Your people could not stand the thought of the despised yellow bellies taking gold that they might have. The persecution started. If our claims showed color, they were jumped. The courts would not uphold our titles. If we resisted, we were driven out of camp. How many of us were killed will never be known. There was nobody to punish our murderers. We are vermin, Mister Anders, lower than the ones you call greaser and nigger, lower than the most miserable mongrel dog in your camps. Do you know what happened here on Chinese Moving Day?"

"I saw Tin Pan," Anders said.

"A man who merely lost his tongue got off easy," Charlie said. "Some drunken Pike started the rumor that the Chinese were pilfering the sluice boxes at the Golden Monte. There was soon a mob. They burned us out. They shot at us as we ran from our shacks. It was winter. Many froze to death before they could reach Caloma or Shingle Springs."

"How did you have the nerve to come back?"

Charlie stirred his tea. "The miners have a thirst for my gin. It gives me a peculiar immunity."

Anders was still thinking of Kettle Corey. He asked: "What did your people live on when they were here, Charlie? They weren't all doing laundry."

"We have been reduced to working the tailings or the diggings abandoned by everyone else," Charlie said. "Your people are interested only in the high-grade ore. But a Chinese can live on fifteen cents a day."

Abandoned diggings. It brought a new thought to Anders. "You spoke of the first years, Charlie. How many shafts were sunk in those years?"

"Who knows? Hundreds. . . ."

"And who'd remember them all now? Only the people still working them. The people who stayed on after everyone else had deserted them. Forgotten them. Back in some forgotten cañon, along some forgotten creek . . ." Anders leaned forward. "Those shafts had to have hoists. There's cable in them, isn't there? Is that what Kettle wanted?"

Charlie smiled. "You have an Oriental mind, Mister Anders. Everything to its logical conclusion."

"Or maybe the conclusion you wanted me to reach," Anders said. He leaned back, the excitement fading, supplanted once again by suspicion. "Why should Kettle want that wire?"

"To keep you from getting it?"

Anders studied the Chinese narrowly. He did not trust the man, yet he could not suppress the growing excitement in him.

205

"Charlie," he said, "if there's wire up there, you'll show me where."

Charlie sipped his tea. "May I apologize, Mister Anders. I could not leave my business here. The miners . . . my gin. . . ."

Anders hated to use the threat. It had outraged him to think of the Pikes cutting out Tin Pan's tongue. He hated to identify himself, however distantly, with such barbarity. Yet he had the angry feeling that this smiling mandarin was toying with him. His patience had run out. He had to have that wire and Charlie knew it.

"Charlie," he said, "do you know what would happen if the miners got the idea you were behind this attempt to keep them from getting water?"

Charlie's face did not change expression. He set his cup down carefully. It made a faint rattle in the saucer. The girl stirred in the corner, whimpering. Charlie breathed a sigh. "Very well, Mister Anders. I will help you."

XIII

Anders took Charlie with him back to the hotel. The party was still going on upstairs but the clerk at the desk said Mason and his daughter had already left. Anders went to the boarding house. Mason was in bed but not yet asleep. When

Anders told them his idea, both Opal and Mason grew excited.

"You think it'll work?" the old man asked. "None of those early shafts could be over two or three hundred feet."

"We'll have to splice. I've thought of that. It's not the best, but I think I can make it hold."

"You'll need some help. I'll send Eddie and Cousin Jack with you. . . ."

"I'd rather not have Cousin Jack."

Mason stared at Anders, his gaunt face darkening. "Anders, you aren't still harboring that crazy notion . . . you can't still believe . . . dammit, Anders, Jack is like a son to me."

"Mister Mason, I don't want to say anything more. I've got to do it my way, that's all."

Mason fussed and fumed, but finally agreed. He scrawled authorization for pack mules and enough grub for a week. Then Opal told him he had to get to sleep and went into the parlor with Anders, closing the bedroom door softly. Opal asked Charlie to find Eddie Norris. When he left, she turned to Anders. There was a strange look to her face. Her lips were soft, slack-looking. It made them seem even riper than he had remembered. Her voice was low and husky.

"I'm sorry for what happened . . . I mean . . . at the hotel."

He smiled wryly. "Not the first time."

"I can't understand Jamaica. If a man loved me

that much . . . two years, following me halfway around the world. The way she treats you . . . she has no right."

"It wasn't always that way, Opal. The woman you saw tonight wasn't the woman I followed halfway around the world." He smiled again. "Maybe she's not the only one," he said lightly. "But what about Eddie?"

She looked at him a moment before she understood what he meant. She colored, shaking her head impatiently. "I don't mean to treat him that way . . . but sometimes he makes me so mad. He's so clumsy, Glenn, he's still a little boy. . . ."

"Give him a chance. He'll grow up. I thought you were engaged."

"Oh, he's asked me. I never actually said anything. Everybody just takes it for granted. I don't know . . . how can you marry a child . . . ?" She broke off, looking directly at him. "You think that's silly, don't you? You think of me as just a child, too."

"When I first saw you," he said, "I thought that you were the kind of woman I should have married."

She touched her lips. All the poise left her and she looked completely vulnerable. For the first time he understood the expression on her face and knew he had made a mistake.

"I kept watching you all evening," she said. Her voice had a breathless, trembling quality. "I thought you must have found out by now . . . the thing you were following . . . a mistake . . . not what you remembered. You know, Glenn, don't you? You know now."

"No, Opal," he said, "I don't know."

She looked at him a long time. She settled back. Finally she said: "You didn't mean it . . . about me."

"I meant it," he said gently. "But not that way."

She was silent again. She took a long breath. When she spoke, her voice was barely audible. "Will you kiss me . . . Glenn?"

"Opal, don't you understand?"

"I understand, Glenn. Will you kiss me?"

He saw that she did understand. He saw a resignation in her eyes. He saw a womanhood that had not been there before. He bent his head and kissed her on the lips. Perhaps they had both meant it to be a good-bye kiss, the last token of something that might have been. But it changed. Maybe it was her nearness. Maybe it was the hunger for a woman built up over two years of wandering and loneliness.

Anders pulled her hard against him. He could feel the softness of her breasts, the tremor that ran through her. He kissed her with bruising force. She moaned and her fingers dug into his back.

"Glenn," she said. "Glenn, Glenn, Glenn . . ."

The door opened behind them. Anders turned

to see Eddie Norris standing there. When Opal finally spoke, her voice sounded strained, husky.

"At least you could have knocked," she said.

"Next time why don't you lock it?" Eddie said. His face was crimson and his eyes burned with a youthful fury.

"Eddie," Anders said. "It wasn't what it looked like."

"Get somebody else for your trip," Eddie said.

He sent Opal a malevolent look and stalked down the hall. Anders started after him, but Opal caught his arm. He stood, looking at her, not knowing what to say. He was still shaken by the moment of passion, more deeply than he cared to admit. He felt a confused sense of guilt and was angry at himself for feeling it.

"I'm sorry, Opal," he said.

Her chin lifted and she looked defiantly into his eyes. "I'm not."

Charlie was waiting in the hall, hands in his sleeves, smiling blandly. Anders took him downstairs and found Dusty in a bunkroom with a dozen other snoring men. The little Duck grumbled and complained but finally got dressed and joined them. They found the storekeeper and bribed him to open up so they could get their supplies. They had to wake Grey at the stables and he made them saddle their own animals.

Anders couldn't forget Opal, as he pushed the two men through the night. He tried to tell himself it had been nothing but a normal reaction—after being so long without a woman. It meant nothing more. It couldn't mean anything more.

Charlie was taking them into the wilderness northeast of Hangtown, country Anders had not seen before. After sunup, as they were crossing a nameless creek where the high bank had been washed away by some placer operations, Charlie asked Anders to look at the soil.

"Would you say there is any value left to it, Mister Anders?"

Anders looked dubiously at the bank. "I don't know mining, Charlie."

"Is not an engineer versed in geology?"

Anders dismounted and kicked experimentally at the remains of the bank. "Isn't it Tertiary gravels they look for?"

The Chinese nodded. "The gold is concentrated in gravels laid down by the ancient rivers. Through the centuries the rivers washed much débris over this bedrock. Sometimes it is hundreds of feet deep. This auriferous material has to be washed away to get at the gold."

"They did a good job here," Anders said. "I don't see much Tertiary left, and certainly no quartz."

Charlie nodded again, more to himself. "I had the same opinion."

Anders looked curiously at him. "I didn't know you were a miner, Charlie."

"I am an ex-stagecoach conductor, Mister Anders, who makes cheap gin."

Later that day they came to the first Chinese camp. They followed a deep gorge to a place where the American miners, deserting their diggings, had left a group of scrofulous log buildings huddled against a towering rock wall. Beside the buildings was a graveyard of rusting machinery, imported during the first insane years, later found to be useless. The season had not started yet for the Americans. The snow that had not yet melted and the blizzards still to come and the bitter cold would keep the Yankees out of their diggings for a few more weeks. But there were a few Chinese already working this abandoned claim.

They had the Chili mill in operation. The huge millstone lay flat in its bed, turning all day on a horizontal shaft, crushing the ore and separating the gold from the quartz. Instead of the mule that usually pulled the wheel a pair of coolies in primitive rope harness plodded the endless circle. And instead of ore cars running on a track from mine to mill, the Chinese were carrying their earth in the ancient way. A line of coolies marched to the mill. Each bore a long pole across his shoulders with a basket of ore hanging from either end. When they reached the Chili mill, the ore was dumped into a chute that carried it beneath the crushing wheel, and the men returned for another load.

Anders was surprised to see that they were not coming from the mouth of the mine that pierced the cañon wall but were carrying the ore from tailings that made miniature mountains beside the original Yankee workings.

"Your people are full of impatience," Charlie said. "They only work the main vein, and when it pinches out, they move on. If the rock doesn't yield them five dollars a yard, they do not bother with it. These Chinese have been re-crushing the tailings for years now. If the Hangtown bullies knew how much they had salvaged, they would come up and take the diggings away from them."

Charlie introduced Anders to the company agent, a stringy Chinese yellow as jaundice in dirty cotton rags who could speak no English. He took them into the deserted adit. A hundred feet inside the horizontal tunnel they came to the shaft. On the platform at its side was a small hoist engine. The cable on the windlass was rusty and blackened, but the sight of it sent a thrill of triumph through Anders.

There wasn't much wire left on the crank. Apparently the mine cage had been left at the bottom of the shaft. They couldn't get the engine started. They had to rig a hand windlass. The company agent gave them some coolies to help, but it took them the rest of the day to get the cage up. When they unwound the cable, they found that it was less than a hundred feet long. Dusty did not try to hide the bitter disappointment in his face.

That night in camp he talked with Anders alone. "Guv'ner, are you sure it will work? It'll take us weeks to get enough cable this way."

Anders turned away to hide his own doubts. He was exhausted and he ached all over from the work. The night was bitterly cold and he couldn't seem to stop shivering, no matter how close to the fire he sat. It was the dark time, when a man's confidence was frozen out of him, and he thought the load would break him.

"Maybe the next shaft'll be deeper," he said. "In the meantime, what do you think of Hangtown Charlie?"

"A man that talks like a coolie one day and a college professor the next? I don't trust him."

"Then you won't object to standing watch with me. Four off and four on, Dusty. And keep one hand warm for your gun."

The next day they moved up the cañon. A creek coursed its bottom, choked with ice. Near noon the men reached another area where the Yankees had left the creek and pierced the cañon wall with adits to follow a vein back into the mountain. They found two more vertical shafts with hoists and some cable. From the Chinese working the abandoned diggings they learned of more cable farther east.

Sooner than he had hoped Anders had enough wire for his bridge. Before the end of the week they were able to start back to Satan's Keyhole, the cable coiled and packed on their mules. In Strawberry Valley the trail forked. Their halted horses stamped and fiddled, stirring up an orange-rind smell from the crushed pine needles.

"The left fork will take me back to Hangtown," Charlie said. He put his hands in his sleeves and bowed his head. Anders could not tell if it was sarcasm in his voice, or humility. "With your permission, Mister Anders."

"Thanks for the help, Charlie," Anders said. "I'll see that Mason's company pays you for your time."

"They will pay." Charlie's smile closed his eyes. "More than they realize."

Anders watched the man turn down trail, a bizarre and incongruous figure in his buffalo coat and bamboo hat. Anders shook his head, trying to rid himself of suspicion and apprehension. He reined his horse toward the left fork.

They reached the Keyhole the next day. They found Garrett Mason waiting for them. With Mason were Cousin Jack, Eddie Norris, and a stranger.

"Opal fought like a catamount," Mason said. "But I knew you'd need all the help you could get if you came back with the wire, and I was going crazy setting around that room all day anyway. I dug up a man who says he can splice your wire for you. He's been working the stamp mills at Grass Valley."

The man's name was Albert Nevis, a thin, hollow-faced consumptive in a shabby suit, boiled shirt, and string tie. Anders shook his hand. It was thin and sensitive, yet held surprising strength.

"You don't work on wire in the stamp mills," Anders said.

"I spent some time in Birmingham," Nevis said.

"We haven't got any machines."

"Maybe your blacksmith can improvise one. If he can't, I think we can still make do."

Nevis turned away to cough weakly. It was like a death rattle deep in his bony chest. Anders glanced at Norris. The young man met his eyes sullenly, colored and looked at the ground. Anders glanced at Cousin Jack, standing to one side, a sullen rogue bull ostracized from the herd.

"It's all right, Anders," Mason said in a low voice. "He won't interfere with you, if that's how you want it. But I couldn't keep him from coming with me."

While Nevis worked on the cable, Anders put in his time with the crews, finishing the piers and making the big hand windlass to wind the cable

216

on. He did not have time to worry about Cousin Jack. He was absorbed in his work now, looking ahead, planning the bridge. His mind was filled with shearing strength and modulus of elasticity, the ultimate resistance to tension when the strength is not axial, the specific gravity of water and pine and granite and cast iron.

The trip up had exhausted Garrett Mason and he spent much of his time resting in the engineer's shack. The men worked willingly enough, but Anders sensed a subtle change occurring in them. He could not look over his shoulder without seeing one of them watching him. And though Cousin Jack stayed with Mason most of the time, playing twenty-one or poker in the shack, his presence lay like a shadow over the work.

When the cable was finished, they shot a line across the chasm and used it to drag the spliced wire to the other side. The cable was then made fast to its saddles on the piers. Before they could begin the superstructure, a blizzard howled down out of the high country and kept them in the cabins for a week. The pressure of confinement wore nerves thin. There was a shooting. Anders had to break up half a dozen fights every day. There was so much hostility between him and Eddie and Cousin Jack that Mason suggested they move into one of the barracks—poker and twenty-one and old sledge, quarts of coffee and tea, the wind slamming snow and sleet against the cabins in a twenty-four hour barrage.

On the morning that the storm abated, they found the drifts piled to the eaves and had to shovel their way out. Anders worked with the men, clearing the trails they would use between camp and the bridge. When he had finished, he saw Mason standing alone at the edge of the cañon, staring across at the glittering wall of icy rocks on the other side. Anders joined him. It was near freezing and the old man was wrapped to the eyes in his greatcoat and scarf. Anders stood beside him, hands buried in his Mackinaw pockets. Their breath turned to milky steam as it left their mouths.

At last Mason said: "You don't know what this means to me, Anders. I thought I'd lost."

"We're not out of the woods yet," Anders said.

"I think you're wrong about that Chinaman," Mason said.

Anders said: "If Hangtown doesn't get this water, half the miners that ever tied two Chinamen together by their pigtails will be out of a job."

"Admitted the Chinese have been given terrible treatment, Anders. But they wouldn't take this kind of revenge. They're a passive people."

"The trail's got to lead somewhere, and Hangtown Charlie was as far as I got," Anders said. Mason did not answer. On the far edge of the gorge the sun was turning the rocks to diamond gargoyles. After a while Anders asked: "What day is it?"

"Sunday, I think."

Anders took out his watch and began to wind it with the key dangling from his Dickens chain.

"That's a handsome turnip," Mason said.

"My father's. Seven-day watch. Out here I keep forgetting."

"Why don't you wind it Friday nights? Payday was always easy for me to remember."

"Sunday was easier for me. I used to wind it just before I went to church."

"I didn't know you were that God-fearing, Anders."

"Well, maybe I was. With Jamaica . . . I guess we got out of the habit."

"She changed a lot of things for you," Mason said. The man was looking at Anders shrewdly. "I had mixed feelings about you in Hangtown, Anders. I liked the way you talked. But there was something wrong. You seemed confused whenever I saw you, unsure of yourself. You couldn't seem to make decisions. A man can't handle a big job in that state of mind. I noticed it most after you had seen your wife." Mason paused. "Up here it's been different. I've watched you work. You know what you're doing."

Anders realized it was true. There had been no time to dwell on Jamaica, no thought of past failures, no hesitancy or indecision.

"You're a damn' good engineer," Mason said. "Don't let her take that from you, Glenn."

Anders did not answer. It was curious. He had not thought of it in those terms before.

Mason cleared his throat. "If those hooligans are this late every morning, we'll never get the job done," he said.

Anders glanced at camp. The crew was still gathered about the barracks. Their voices reached Anders in a restless murmur. He and Mason walked back to camp.

"I hate to make you work on Sunday," he told them, "but you know how precious time is now. Thaw's due any day. We're weeks behind schedule."

"We don't mind the Sunday work," Quill said.

"Then let's get the jury rig ready," Anders said. "We'll lower the first section of beams this morning."

None of them moved. They seemed to be looking toward Sluefoot. The Pike took out his Henry Clay. He bit off a chaw and the odor of licorice and molasses turned the air sweet.

"I dunno," Sluefoot said, chewing thoughtfully. "If these piers is the same kind as that bridge at San Felipe, and it give way beneath a platoon of soldiers . . ."

"What does a pick-and-panner like you know about San Felipe?" Anders asked. "That was ten years ago in Spain. And some fool lieutenant didn't know enough to make his column change to route step when they hit the bridge. You won't have any conditions like that here."

"There warn't no soldiers at Mast Hope," Sluefoot said.

Anders felt his face go stiff. In the silence, in the achingly cold air, the random shifting of feet on the ground made sharp little sounds. Anders looked around till he saw Cousin Jack, standing alone by the engineer's shack. He returned Anders's gaze sullenly.

"You told me you hadn't been in the bridge business long, Sluefoot," Anders said.

"Never built one before," Sluefoot said.

Anders was still looking at Cousin Jack. "Where did you hear about San Felipe and Mast Hope, Sluefoot?"

"I can't recall."

"Then how about that jury rig?"

"I ain't swingin' out on no cable a thousand feet above the ground."

"Those cables will hold," Nevis said. "I've spliced 'em on longer stretches than this."

None of them moved. They wouldn't meet Anders's eyes. They fingered their faces and stamped their numbed feet. Anders knew he might bully them into the job. But it would not remove the poison of doubt and mistrust planted in their minds by the story of his failure on the Mast Hope bridge.

"Guv'ner's asking you to go out there," Cousin Jack said. "Ain't got the guts to do it himself."

It surprised Anders to hear the man speak. He glanced sharply at the Cornishman. There was a jeering tone to Cousin Jack's voice, a smoldering mockery in his eyes. Anders was sure now that it had been Jack who told them about San Felipe and Mast Hope.

"Put the jury rig on the cables," Anders said. "I'll tie in the first section."

The men looked surprised. Then Dusty cackled and scooped a coil of hemp off the ground, heading toward the pier. One by one the others followed. They slung the ropes over the cable next to the saddles. They hung the temporary platform and loaded it with tie rods and iron straps and tools. Anders stepped aboard and they slowly let the platform slide down the dip in the cable. He raised a hand when he was far enough away to drop the first section of main beam.

There was a wind coming up the cañon and the cables were creaking mournfully as they swayed. The gorge yawned a thousand feet below. Ice gleamed on its rocky walls in the pale morning light. He felt a sharp giddiness. He swung his eyes quickly upward. He knew an insidious reluctance to release his grip on the ropes. The men were preparing to lower the first section of beam out to him and he had to start work.

He fumbled bolts and tie rod off the floor of the

platform and raised up to fasten the rod in place on the cable. The platform began to shake in the wind. He had to chip ice from the cable before he could get his bolts in place. It was a job for two men. He was reaching up to slip the tie rod onto its bolt when his foot slipped.

He dropped the rod. He caught wildly at the ropes. He heard the shout from the men. He hung against the ropes, watching the tie rod turn over and over as it fell into the cañon.

"Want to come back in, Anders?" Cousin Jack called.

Anders cursed the man. He got another rod and climbed back up to attach it. He gave them the signal and they lowered the first length of pine beam. Its end crashed onto the platform. The whole jury rig jerked and tilted.

The straps and rod connections were already bolted onto the beam. All Anders had to do was attach the tie rods. His fingers were numb. He dropped a bolt. He cut himself and could not feel the pain. The wind whined mournfully down the cañon. It buffeted the platform. It pushed Anders playfully.

He finally got the connection made. They dropped the parallel beam out to him. He connected it to the cable and they swung the tie beam out on a rope. When he had it connected, he looked up to see the men watching closely. He knew what was in their minds.

As more beams and rods were added, the weight of the structure itself would increase. Inevitably the men would have to put their own weight on the beams. Actually the suspension bridge's weight was a much smaller factor than that of a bridge supported by trestles. But these men had never worked with suspension before. They had already seen their trestle bridge collapse three times.

Anders stepped off the platform onto the beam, hanging to the tie rod. He had to shout to be heard above the wind. "You've got a shearing strength of over four tons to the square inch here. The whole bunch of you could line up on this beam."

"What about the wind?" Cousin Jack shouted. "It's going to play hell with your stresses."

"I've accounted for that. You'll have enough diagonals to buck any pull."

Still the men hung back. Their blind ignorance angered Anders. Cousin Jack's constant hostility angered him. He began to jump up and down on the beam.

"What's the matter with you?" he shouted. "You'd trust beams like this in a mine! If they'll hold up a mountain, they'll hold up a man! They'll hold up a *hundred* men!"

He saw that the graphic illustration was having some effect. The men glanced at each other, grinning sheepishly. Quill started hesitantly for the pier. Seeing that their resistance was breaking, Garrett Mason climbed onto the pier, waving his arm.

"Come on. If we don't get this job done, there won't be any use going back to your mines."

"Mister Mason!" Cousin Jack shouted. He ran toward the pier. "No, Mister Mason . . . wait . . . !"

Anders did not realize what Mason intended until it was too late. The old man let himself stiffly off the pier onto the beam. Anders was still jumping up and down on it. There was a shrieking crack at his end. Then there was nothing beneath him.

His right hand slid down the tie rod. When it reached the end, the weight of his falling body almost tore his grip loose. His shoulder was wrenched in its socket as his body twisted against the arm.

He hung in mid-air for an instant, shouting with pain, not even knowing that his grip had held. He saw Mason far beneath him, twisting and turning as he fell into the cañon, a swiftly diminishing miniature, a little rag doll.

Still dangling, Anders swung his left arm up and caught the tie rod. The platform was yawing and pitching in the wind. He couldn't swing himself aboard. All he could do was hang on while they hauled the platform back to the pier.

With agonizing slowness the gap between platform and cliff shortened. He saw the beam hanging from the pier. It was tied to the pier on a swivel connection that would allow the beam to rise and fall with the movement of the bridge. When the beam had sheared off at Anders's end, it had swung down against the cliff and the shock had apparently thrown Mason free.

As the platform reached the cliff, the wind tilted it violently, almost shaking Anders loose. He was slammed against the cliff. He felt his numb fingers slip on the tie rod.

"Climb up!" Quill shouted. "We can't git you any closer!"

Anders tried to swing himself onto the platform of the jury rig. The wind tore him away. He didn't have the strength to fight it. His hands were numb. His grip was going. He looked into the shadowy depths of the gorge. His fingers slipped on the tie rod again. Panic gagged him.

He saw Tin Pan climb off the pier. The Chinese cook was white with fear. Anders could see it in every quaking line of his skinny body. But he shinnied down the beam with a rope. He snaked the noose over Anders's head, under his arms. Anders couldn't hold on any longer.

He felt his hands slide loose of their grip and he plunged into empty air. He fell ten feet before the rope caught him. It tore at his armpits, squeezed the air from him in a gasp. He dangled helplessly against the cliff, spinning in the wind.

They tied the rope on the windlass and cranked him up. At the edge of the cliff Quill and Tin Pan pulled him to safety. He crouched on his hands and knees, spent and dizzy. He saw that some of the men had already started down the trail. Cousin Jack led them, far ahead of the others.

When Anders had enough strength, he started down after them. It was a long hike. By the time Anders got to the bottom, Cousin Jack had already reached Garrett Mason's crumpled body. He was crouched over it on both knees, his head bowed.

As Anders came off the steep trail and crossed the boulder-strewn cañon, Cousin Jack rose. His eyes were blank and there was a wild, loose look to his face.

"Mister Mason!" he cried. It was not a human sound. It was the crazed roar of some animal in pain. "God damn you, Anders! Mister Mason."

Cousin Jack's shaggy bearskin coat made him look like some nightmarish monster, as he rushed at Anders. It caught Anders completely off guard. He tried to evade the man in the last moment.

But Cousin Jack crashed against him. His hands clawed Anders's face. His wild blows rocked the engineer's body.

Anders tried to wheel free, tried to protect himself. He caught one of the blows on an arm, striking for the man. The bear coat was a cushion. His fist had no effect. One of the Cornishman's wild swings cracked him across the face. It rocked his head and he went blind with shock.

He stumbled backward and another blow struck him, knocking him off his feet. He rolled over. A savage pain stabbed through his ribs. He knew Cousin Jack was kicking him. He tried to rise. The man kicked him again.

It knocked him flat. He was stunned. He couldn't rise. He tried to crawl away. A kick caught him in the ribs and flopped him over. He hugged his arms over his face, trying to protect it. He had seen a man stamped to death on the railroad. He knew that was what Cousin Jack intended now. He couldn't stop it. He was stunned and sickened and he didn't have the strength to stop him. The kicks jarred him and the pain made bright flashes before his eyes and he made coughing sounds and thrashed in a wild, futile effort to escape.

He was on his back when he had a dim glimpse of Eddie Norris stepping in behind Cousin Jack and clubbing him with a gun. It dazed the Cornishman. He bent forward, made a wheezing sound. He wheeled halfway around, kicking again at Anders, almost in reflex.

Norris caught his grizzly coat, pulling him back and hitting again. It drove Cousin Jack to one knee. He lunged erect again, almost instantly. But the blow had stunned him. The blind look was in his eyes. He didn't seem to see Norris. He made no attempt to get at Anders again. He put his hands to his face and plunged away from them.

"Mister Mason," he said. "Mister Mason . . . !"
It came from him in a weird wail. Anders had never heard a man make such a sound. He walked like a drunk, blindly, stumbling, veering back and forth. He kept calling for Mason.

"Cousin Jack!" Norris called. The man did not seem to hear him. "Stop him, somebody," Norris said.

The men made no move. They watched the man stumble up the cañon, his hands to his eyes now, making the frightening sounds. Norris took a few steps, then stopped, looking helplessly after him. Anders groaned and got to one knee. Norris looked at him.

"Thanks, Eddie," Anders said.

The young man's face was sick and gray, and there was a miserable accusation in his eyes. "Don't thank me," he said.

XIV

It was raining the day they brought Garrett Mason's body into Hangtown. They had met the storm the second day on the trail. They had come down out of a land of ice and snow into a land of rain and mud. It meant another snowstorm behind them—another blizzard in the high country—maybe the last of the season.

Main Street was a bog. The clapboard shacks

and log buildings were black-wet. Window light made yellow smears in the shimmering wall of water. A single freight wagon stood on the street. The heads of its sixteen mules were bowed low, their ears plastered down like dishrags. The rain did a crystal dance on slanting roof tops and in the hundred miniature rivers of the wheel ruts. The sound of it was a muffled rattle and a sodden roar. Anders had been listening to it for ten hours.

He halted his horse before the Riley boarding house. Beside him was Garrett Mason wrapped in a tarp and tied on his horse. Behind Mason rode Dusty and Eddie Norris.

Most of the crew had left camp before Anders. He knew they had reached Hangtown ahead of him and were probably in the saloons and deadfalls now, telling the story. It filled Anders with a haunting sense of guilt.

He looked back at the men. Dusty seemed oblivious to the rain. It beat relentlessly down on his wool hat, rattling the brim and filling it with water and pouring off on his shoulders and down the collar of his coat. He sat stooped in the saddle, staring emptily at Mason's dead body. The rainwater shimmering on his cheeks looked like tears.

Anders said: "Get him under that lean-to, Dusty, out of the rain. Eddie and I had better go upstairs first." The little man did not respond, and Anders said sharply: "Dusty?"

230

The Duck looked up, as though in surprise. Anders had to repeat the order. Like an automaton Dusty took the reins of Mason's horse and led it toward the shed beside the boarding house.

Anders and Norris went upstairs. The young man had said very little during the trip. He stood looking sickly at the door a long time before he knocked. Opal answered. She started to smile when she saw them. The expression on their faces stopped her. She put a hand softly to her mouth and backed into the room. They followed her. Eddie's fists were clenched at his sides and muscle made little ridges beneath the gray flesh along his jaw. He looked at Anders.

"Opal," Anders said. He paused, sick. "Opal . . ."

"Dad," she said. She made a moaning sound and then cried out sharply, running against Anders, trying to get past him and through the door.

He held her, saying miserably: "It won't do any good, Opal, it won't do any good."

She looked at Eddie. Her face was parchment stretched to the tearing point. Her mouth was open but she could seem to make no sound. Her eyes had the same blind, wild look Anders had seen in Cousin Jack's eyes.

Eddie held out his hands, taking Opal from Anders. She buried her face against his chest, allowing him to hold her for a moment. Then she made a broken sound and tore free. She walked across the room. She spread her hands out against the window and looked out into the darkness.

"Dad?" she said. "Daddy?"

She whimpered. She put her hands over her eyes and turned around and went down into the wing chair. Her face was buried against its back and her legs were curled under her and it make her look like a little girl huddled in the big chair. She began to shake uncontrollably.

Anders felt like a man on the rack. "Opal," he said. "There was no reason for it . . . that beam had a shearing strength of over four tons to the square inch . . . there was just no reason. . . ."

"You'd better get out," Eddie said.

"Eddie, for God's sake. . . ."

"You'd better get out, Anders!"

The boy's voice was savage. His fists were opening and closing spasmodically. Anders looked back at Opal. She was still shaking violently. Filled with an immense helplessness, he left them.

Downstairs he saw a group of dripping miners in the parlor. They were roomers at the boarding house. They had carried Mason inside, still wrapped in his soaked tarpaulin, and had laid him on the settee. Mrs. Riley was with them, a wet wrapper over her head. She cursed Anders in Gaelic.

"Ah, ye Firbolg, ye black and grovelin' Firbolg. Knew it, I did, the first time I laid eyes on ye. Tell

Opal, I did. The breath of evil on him, sez I . . . smell it I could . . . a Shan muck that'll bring ye nothin' but sorrow, a black and grovelin' Firbolg, even if his head is yellow. . . ."

Anders turned away from her. He saw Dusty standing near the door, staring apathetically at the canvas-wrapped corpse. He went to the man.

"Dusty . . . the arrangements . . . will you take care of him?"

For a while he did not think the Duck had heard. Finally Dusty nodded.

Anders went outside, stopping beneath the overhang. The rain roared against the wooden awning and made a constant drizzle through the cracks. Anders still ached all over from the beating Cousin Jack had given him. He was soaking wet. He was thoroughly used up, emotionally and physically. He had no idea what he intended to do, where he could go. There wasn't one of them who didn't seem to blame him for Mason's death. It was like a pressure against him. He knew a frantic need to escape. Yet he knew there would be no escape.

And why should they blame him? Why should he feel such guilt? Some flaw in the beam, the one time in a thousand. How could he have known? Mason had been putting his faith in just such beams for a lifetime. They all had.

He looked out into the dismal rain. It made him think of Cousin Jack out there somewhere, crazed

233

with grief over Mason's death. The Cornishman had not showed up again in camp. But Anders felt that he had not seen the last of the man. Cousin Jack, more than any of them, blamed Anders.

Anders saw the horses, still standing dolefully in the downpour. He mounted his paint and led the others up the street into the shelter of Grey's barn. Grey came out of his tack room. Tired as he was, Anders helped the man unsaddle and rub the animals down. Grey didn't say much, but Anders saw the man looking at him. Finally he said: "You heard?"

"Sluefoot," Grey said. "Pulled in about half an hour ahead of you."

Anders went back out into the rain. The pressure was growing in him. Cousin Jack at Downieville—Kettle Corey on the Mountain House Grade—Barton—all leading up to that tarp-wrapped body in Mrs. Riley's boarding house, all crying for an answer. And the last time the trail had led to Hangtown Charlie.

Anders went down Caloma to Hangtown Creek. The creek was over its banks now, washing through some of the burned, deserted shacks huddling around the dump heaps. Hangtown Charlie's building was on high enough ground to escape the flood. Someone inside was plucking a lute. It had an ancient, dissonant sound, like no music Anders had ever heard. He drew his gun and knocked heavily on the door. He heard whispered voices inside, someone scurrying around.

"Charlie," he said, "it's Anders. Let me in. Unless you want me to kick your door down."

In a moment the girl unbarred the door and opened it.

Hangtown Charlie sat on his mat on the floor. He had on a mandarin robe of yellow silk, embroidered with fantastic black dragons. The girl went back to crouch in a corner, the lute in her lap. Neither of them seemed surprised.

Hangtown Charlie smiled humorlessly. "My house is yours, Mister Anders."

The room was smoky with incense. It made Anders's eyes water. He walked toward Charlie.

"Charlie, I've had it up to the neck. Mason is dead. I'm going to find out who's behind it."

"From what I understand, the deed was yours."

"I don't know what happened. All I know is I've taken all I mean to. Prove to me you're not behind it, Charlie. Right now. Prove to me you're not to blame. If you don't, I think I'll kill you."

Charlie sighed. "I do not think you can kill me, any more than you could have put me at the mercy of the miners by telling them I was responsible for keeping their water from them."

Anders felt himself sway a little. He made a hopeless sound, and let the gun sag. He began coughing in the smoke.

"If you weren't afraid of my threat," he said, "why did you help me get that wire?"

"Because I thought our ultimate goal might be the same," Charlie said.

Anders frowned at him. He wiped his watering eyes. "Will you put out that damned incense?" he said.

Charlie waved a hand and the girl put the lute down and crawled across the room to the little copper brazier that stood in front of a lacquered bamboo screen. She snuffed the incense. The smell sickened Anders. He put his gun away and walked to the mat. The water in his boots made a squishing sound. The water dripped off his hat and off his Mackinaw and formed growing puddles on the floor. He sat down. He closed his eyes. Exhaustion swept over him like an overpowering weight.

"Well," he said, "are you going to play Confucius for a while or are you going to tell me?"

"Will you finish the bridge?" Charlie asked.

"What with? Who'll hold the water company together? It was Mason's baby. The men wouldn't go back. Too many failures, Charlie. You couldn't find one miner in the whole Lode that would climb out on that cable now. . . ."

Anders broke off, realizing it was the first time he had given voice to his defeat, realizing how hopelessly it had poured out of him. He felt purged. There was a sense of finality about putting it into words.

"You could not by-pass Satan's Keyhole?" Charlie asked.

"It would take another year to flume around it. They wouldn't have tried bridging if there was another way."

Charlie was silent. Finally he said: "You were right about the Six Companies. Their commercial interests are more varied than the real estate in San Francisco. I am an agent for the Kong Chow Company. For a long time they have been trying to get into mining. Not the miserable, one-man, riverbank claims from which we are driven as soon as we find any real gold. It would have to be a big operation, big enough to withstand Chinese Moving Day and the other things that have always destroyed our chances up here. When the Golden Monte was offered, Kong Chow was first to bid."

It was a complete surprise to Anders. "Why should Golden Monte want to sell? It's the richest mine on the American."

"There is Eastern capital in the corporation. The failure of Mason Water to complete their flumes has made Golden Monte stock drop dangerously. They feel it has become too big a gamble to hang on. If water is not brought this year, the bottom will drop out."

"Why should it? The gold is still there."

"It would take ten times as long to get the old way. And time means money. It seems that Eastern stockholders do not appreciate the practical aspects. All they can see is the quotations on those certificates. And the quotations are going down. Victor Castine got his order to sell, and he must do so. It is a big chance for the Chinese."

"Do you really think you could hold it? Even such a big mine?"

"The Six Companies are a powerful force, Mister Anders. The Missouri Pikes and Texas bullies will find that they are not dealing with a few miserable coolies in one of these little Chinatowns. And the governor has promised support from the militia should we need it."

"That's what you were doing at the Golden Monte?" Anders said.

Charlie nodded. "I am supposed to inspect the mine for Kong Chow. But they do not want me to use my credentials unless it is absolutely necessary. We do not want trouble until we have actual possession. If the miners up here find out beforehand, there is no telling what they will do."

"Then you couldn't get in?"

"Not as Hangtown Chollie. But I will get my chance, sooner or later. So far all I have seen is some of the outer placer workings. They have reason for the guards. It is a very rich mine. Can you see now that the Chinese are not behind this trouble with the bridge? They have as much cause as you to want the water to get through."

Anders bowed his head. Suspicion of Charlie had seemed like something tangible, at least. Now he was in a vacuum again. He heard a faint rattle behind him. He turned. The girl was looking at the screen. She looked quickly away. Anders raised his gun and pointed it at the screen.

"Tell them I've got this gun on the screen, Charlie," he said. "Tell them if they don't come out I'm shooting."

Charlie said something in Chinese. The screen swayed. Tin Pan stepped from behind it. Anders stared blankly at the grinning cook.

"When you began knocking, we thought it was some of the miners," Charlie said. "Tin Pan could have got out of the window behind the screen." The cook joined them and sat down. He looked unblinkingly at Anders, grinning like an idiot. Charlie said: "You are his idol, since you saved him from Chileno and that Pike. At the Keyhole, after you left, Tin Pan and Nevis looked at the beam that had given way. It was not broken. It had been sawed."

Anders stared blankly at Tin Pan. The cook nodded vigorously, making incomprehensible signs with his bony hands. Anders cursed softly. Why hadn't he thought to look? He had been too dazed from Jack's beating, too stunned by

Mason's death, too filled with his own sense of guilt.

"Who did it, Tin Pan?"

The cook did not stop grinning, but he shook his head from side to side. Anders hadn't expected him to know. A new suspicion came to him.

Cousin Jack had goaded him to get on the beam and prove its strength. Then Cousin Jack had tried to stop Mason from following Anders out. It was an ugly thought, but it held a logic Anders could not escape. No wonder Cousin Jack had been so crazed at Mason's death. His trap had boomeranged. He had killed Mason himself.

A sound outside made Charlie stop. It was a woman's voice. Calling.

"Anders? Glenn? Glenn . . . ?"

It sounded like Opal's voice. He rose quickly and stepped to the door. Its light made a shimmering path through the pouring rain. Opal Mason stumbled into it. She was bareheaded and wore only a satin cloak over her dress. It was plastered to her body and kept whipping soddenly at her legs and making her trip.

"Cousin Jack!" she panted. "He's in town. Glenn . . ." She stumbled and almost fell. Anders caught her and she hung against him, gasping, spent. "Grey . . . the stableman . . . came to Missus Riley's . . . said Cousin Jack came to the livery just after you did. The condition Jack was in . . . Grey didn't realize it till too late . . . made the mistake . . . told Jack you were here, told him you'd headed toward Charlie's. . . ."

The gunshot made a deafening crash.

The bullet whipped through the flimsy building at his side. He felt Opal go stiff. She wheeled around, her back against him, her body shielding his, one arm thrown across him in an instinctive gesture of protectiveness.

"Jack!" she called. "Don't be a fool . . . !"

The gun crashed again. The bullet struck the thin hide on the window and the hide split lengthwise with a sharp pop. Anders knew they were silhouetted in the doorway. He caught Opal and flung her aside, lunging after her and fighting to get his Mackinaw unbuttoned. He had a dim sense of the shaggy figure running at them from the rain-swept darkness.

He got his Walker out and fired. Cousin Jack returned the shot, firing at the flash of Anders's gun. The bullet struck Anders's Walker and the stunning blow slammed his arm back, smashing his knuckles against the wall and knocking the gun from his numbed fingers.

He cursed and went to one knee, pawing with his left hand for the gun. He couldn't find it in the mud. He could see Cousin Jack now, only a few yards away, plunging at them in the rain. Opal still crouched against the wall beside Anders. He knew he had to get her out of it.

He caught her and shoved her roughly away

from the shack, into the darkness. He lunged after her.

"Anders!" Cousin Jack bawled. He began firing again. Opal stumbled and fell. Anders had to catch her under the arm, dragging her into the muddy heaps of refuse.

He couldn't see Cousin Jack now but he could hear the man splashing through the mud after them. Anders and Opal went at a stumbling run into the maze of wrecked, charred shacks. They halted against a crumbling wall, trying to hear Cousin Jack over their own hoarse breathing and the roar of the rain.

"Head toward the creek," Anders panted. "I'll go up Caloma and lead him off."

"I won't leave you," she said fiercely.

"Opal . . . he's out of his head. . . ."

"I won't leave you."

"Anders!" Cousin Jack yelled. "God damn you, Anders!"

They could hear him crashing blindly about in the wreckage of the shacks, seeking them out. Anders took Opal's arm again. They stumbled on through the Chinese camp, reaching the steep banks of the creek. They waded through the overflow, going to their waists to cross gullies. They got as far as Studebaker's wheelbarrow shop, stilted on the steep bank. They went in under the stilts, huddling out of the rain, listening for Cousin Jack.

After a long time, Anders said: "I guess it's over now."

She didn't say anything. She put her face against his chest and began to cry softly. It struck Anders that he had never held Jamaica when she cried. He had held her in passion or in anger, but she had never let him hold her when she cried. After a long while, when Opal had quieted down, Anders said: "Opal, I've got to tell you something. That beam . . . I didn't even know it at the time . . . that beam didn't break. It was sawed."

Opal's face was pressed against his chest and it muffled her words so that he could barely understand them. She spoke in a weak, exhausted voice, a voice with all the emotion drained out of it. "I'm glad, Glenn. I mean . . . I want you to know . . . Eddie, Missus Riley, I guess even Dusty, they all seem to blame you for Dad's death, but I want you to know I didn't. Even up in the room . . . the shock, I couldn't help it . . . but I didn't blame you, Glenn, I didn't blame you. . . ." She trailed off. She began to tremble violently. She couldn't stop. He held her hard against him. A touch of hysteria came to her voice. "The beam . . . sawed. Why? Who would do it?"

"Cousin Jack."

"No, he loved Dad. He couldn't. . . ."

"That's just it. He was trying to kill me. He

243

never dreamed your dad would jump out on that beam."

She looked up at him and he could see she was still unable to believe him. "You know how much Jack wanted your dad to stop," Anders said.

"I . . . I suppose so . . . but he *wouldn't* go this far, not Cousin Jack."

"I can't figure it any other way, Opal. He tried everything else to get me out of the way."

She made a soft moaning sound. There was torture in it, and compassion. He realized he felt the same way. He could find no hate in him for the Cornishman, not even anger. Only a sort of bitter pity.

"Well, then he finally got what he wanted," she said.

"How do you mean?"

"The bridge," Opal said. "It won't be finished now."

"You won't have a thing without it, Opal. Every cent your dad had is tied up in it."

"I couldn't ask you to go back, Glenn, not after this."

"Why not?" he asked. "I owe you something. I'd reached the end of a trail. Nobody else was willing to trust me with a job. You gave me a chance to come back. You and your father."

He was surprised to find himself thinking in such terms. Before, he had thought in terms of ambition, had wanted to become an engineer, had catered to his own hungers; he had wanted Jamaica, had thought of his own loss, willing to make any sacrifice to get her back again.

Opal was gripping his arms. "Glenn, I appreciate it . . . you don't know how I appreciate it. But the men . . . you'll never get them back on that bridge."

"I can give it one hell of a try," he said.

XV

Anders took Opal back to the boarding house, then started hunting the men. He remembered Hangtown Charlie saying that Albert Nevis had been with Tin Pan when the cook found out the beam had been sawed. Anders started a tour of the saloons, searching for Nevis. As he moved through the muddy, drenched streets, he kept looking for Cousin Jack, waiting for the man to appear, lurching from the mouth of a side street, from the door of a saloon, the gun in his hand and the wild look in his eyes. It made Ander's shoulder muscles rigid with tension. It made his palms clammy.

He found Nevis bucking the bank in the smoke-filled deadfall called John Fool's Saloon. The man left the table reluctantly, coughing in the smoke. He had to stop outside and lean against the wall, coughing until he retched.

"Stay down here and you'll be dead in a week," Anders said.

The man held his head. "A week, a year, these mountains don't know the difference."

"Tin Pan told me about the beam."

"What good will it do now?" Nevis asked cynically.

"Will you come with me to Barton's?" Anders asked.

Nevis studied him, then nodded indifferently. They went past the hang tree to an outlying shack where the trappers bunked. It was a single room with a clay chimney.

Quill sat as close to the fire as he could get. He had his sleeves pushed back and was rubbing heated bear grease into his elbows. The other two trappers sat at the puncheon table, playing the mountain man's game of old sledge with horsehide cards. Barton lay in one of the bunks hung from the wall by rawhide ropes. Anders told them that the beam had been sawed. He saw the suspicion in their faces and knew they would not have believed him without Nevis to verify it.

"Well," Quill said, "I guess that takes a load off your shoulders."

Anders looked at Barton. The man was mending slowly, but was no longer delirious. Anders asked him if it was Cousin Jack who had shot him and destroyed the flume.

"I still can't recollect a thing," Barton said.

"The last thing I knew was that shot, and a big thump in my ribs, and pitching off the horse. When I come out of it, I was here in the cabin."

Anders looked at the others. "I want you to help me finish the bridge."

"I had my fill," Quill said. "Looks to me like somebody was willin' to kill Mason to stop this job."

"I think it was me they wanted," Anders said.

"Or maybe they just wanted the bridge to go down, they didn't care who was on it," Quill said. "So it might be me next time."

"Barton told me you killed a dozen Utes," Anders said.

Quill rubbed his joints. "That was a long time ago. I'm an old man. If I git too far from the fire, I'll jist stiffen up and die."

"If Mason Water gets through, your stake will be enough to keep you by the fire all the rest of your life," Anders said.

Quill sucked in his cheeks and shook his head. Barton raised feebly on an elbow.

"Damn you for a chicken-hearted Digger Injun, Quill," he said. "Anders saved my miserable life. He went on after you was so crippled up you had to quit. He went on after most men'd give up. He'd do the same for you. If he did, I'd calculate I owed him a debt. What else could it be, when a man saves your pard? If you don't calculate that way, you kin plum forget all the years we set traps together. You can collect your possibles and light a shuck from this here camp."

Quill looked at his greasy hands. He sighed heavily and wiped them on his elk-hide leggings. He groaned and cursed, getting up. He stood rubbing his hip and surveying the other two trappers at the table.

"Well, git off your hunkers," he said. "We ain't gittin' any bridges built this way."

They found Dusty at the boarding house. When Anders told him about the beam, the little Sydney Duck did not say anything. He gazed at Anders with the same apathy that had been in his eyes since Mason's death. Anders cursed him for a damned escaped convict. He said Mason had given him a chance and now Dusty was failing the man. If the water company did not succeed, Opal would be left without a thing. Dusty pulled at his notched ear and did not answer.

Anders set out with Nevis to comb the saloons. He found most of the crew in one deadfall or another. But learning about the beam did not change their attitude. Satan's Keyhole had become a jinx in their minds. They had seen too many failures. They had no more faith in the project, with Mason gone. Near midnight, bitterly discouraged, he went back to Grey's Livery, where he had told the trappers to meet him.

A fire had been built inside the barn and he saw the men huddled around it in their blankets. But there were more than the three trappers. A dozen more—evil-looking little men in striped jerseys and scarred brutes in salt-brined ducks and sallow-faced wharf rats with diseased faces and furtive eyes—all with the notch of the Australian penal colony in their ears. Dusty stood by the fire, proud as a pouter pigeon. Anders realized the man must have gathered every Sydney Duck in camp.

Before Anders could even react, another group of men came out of the night. They came single file, many of them barefoot, shivering in their rags and holding their conical bamboo hats on against the pouring rain. At their head was Tin Pan, grinning and making enthusiastic signals with his skinny yellow hands.

Nevis began to laugh. It brought on his cough again, and he went over to lean against the wall. Anders couldn't tell which was laughing and which was coughing.

"Well, you got your crew," Nevis said. He was still laughing feebly. "The worst dregs from the blackest barrel in the scummiest camp in the Sierras."

XVI

Anders left with his strange crew the next morning. The rain had turned to a drizzle that stayed with them almost all day. Near evening they rose above it. The clouds lay beneath them and they seemed to stand at the shore of a dark and billowing sea that stretched westward as far as they could see and blanketed the mountains through which they had come.

They reached Satan's Keyhole the next evening. Tin Pan took Anders to the beam and the whole crew inspected it. The iron connecting straps, covering two feet of the beam end, hid the saw cut. The cut had gone through a bolt hole, leaving enough wood to support the beam's own weight, but little more.

Anders put his men to work immediately. They carefully inspected all the beams. The cable had been unbolted at the far pier and had dropped into the cañon. It was a precarious job looking at every foot of the cable to make sure Nevis's splices had not been tampered with, before they hauled it up to the pier again.

Anders had his greatest trouble with the Chinese. There was only one company agent with them who could speak English and all the orders had to be issued through him. One of the Sydney

Ducks, a man named Mulligan, turned out to be a blacksmith, and he was put in charge of all the ironwork.

Anders sent Dusty and a small crew he could not spare to repair the section of flume that had been dynamited when Barton was shot. The thaw was on its way. The skin of ice on the water butts was thinner every morning. There was water in the bottom of the cañon from melting snows higher up and the drifts around camp had turned to bogs that filled the camp with the smell of wet earth a million years old.

Anders pushed himself harder than he ever had before. He had to teach every Chinese his job. He had to drive his skeleton crew till each one was doing the work of two or three men. He was out on the bridge most of the day and by nightfall he was so exhausted that he fell asleep over supper.

The superstructure was more than halfway across when Eddie Norris arrived in camp with a dozen men from the old crew. Such an addition was a welcome sight and Anders greeted Eddie happily. But Eddie would not smile.

"I'm sorry I blamed you for Mister Mason's death," the young man said. "I should have known better."

"Forget it," Anders told him. "How about Opal? Do you understand that now, Eddie?"

"I understood it then," Norris said. "I didn't

come back for you or for her, Anders. I signed up for a job and I'm going to finish it."

Anders realized there was no use pressing it. He said: "On that basis, then, take your crew and start the flume on the other side of the cañon. Drive straight toward Hangtown. What mines lie off the main route can bring their own flumes to it. By the time that water's ready to come down, we can carry it clear to Hangtown."

Three days later Dusty returned to report that the upper flume was repaired. He said thaw had reached the high country; they could probably open the head gates any time. Anders had a report from Norris that the mines had supplemented his crew and he expected the lower section of flume to be finished that Friday. On Wednesday, with only fifty feet of bridge left to go, two men representing the mines arrived in camp. They said many mines had completed their flumes to the main canal, their crews were standing by, and they wanted to know when they could go to work. Anders told them they could expect water by the end of the week.

That evening Quill told Anders that someone had seen Cousin Jack watching camp from a ridge.

Anders had lost his own gun at Hangtown Charlie's the night of the rain. He borrowed one from Quill, an old Paterson Colt with a folding trigger. That night he cleaned it carefully and checked the loads.

Mulligan came to him the next morning. The Duck's hands were blackened with soot from his forge and he had a long face. He told Anders they were running out of connecting straps.

"How could you?" Anders said. "I ordered more than enough when we first came up here."

"All I know is they're gone, and we don't have no iron in camp for more. I saw somebody skulkin' about my forge last night, but I thought it was one o' the chinks scavengin'."

Anders cursed softly to himself. He looked off at the black timber and the ridge tops beyond. He was thinking of Cousin Jack. Without those straps the bridge could not be finished.

"How many straps have we got left?" he asked.

Mulligan scowled. "Dozen or so. They'll have 'em used up before noon."

Anders was still looking at the ridges. If Cousin Jack was up there, Anders couldn't approach him without being seen. But there was another way. If Jack saw Anders leave camp, apparently on his way back to Hangtown . . .

Anders told Mulligan to get Dusty and Eddie Norris, then went to the cabin for his coat and more shells for his gun. He was at the corral, saddling a horse when the two men appeared. He told them what he was going to do. They wanted to accompany him.

"We can't afford to slow down the work by taking any key men off the bridge," Anders said. "Besides, if Cousin Jack saw you leave with me, he might not come after the bait. We haven't got any time left. This is the only way I can see to do it."

He left them at the corral and rode down the trail. He passed the promontory and glanced back. The distant bridge was framed in the keyhole shape in the chasm. Satan's Keyhole. He remembered the first time he had heard of it, from Opal, back at Downieville. It seemed a long time ago.

The trail finally cut away from the gorge into timber that hid him from the camp and from the ridges above. About a half a mile ahead of him was a junction with the trail that came in from Strawberry Valley. It crossed the ridges south of camp, and if Cousin Jack was anywhere up there, he could reach it in a short time. If he was racing to catch up with Anders, he would undoubtedly take to the trail rather than fight through the rough timber.

Anders kicked his horse into a hard gallop. In a few minutes the altitude had the animal lathered and laboring. When Anders judged he was near the junction, he turned off into timber. He reached a point at the edge of a high meadow where he could see the junction below. He dismounted and led his horse carefully through the pines till he came upon the Strawberry Valley trail. He could see several hundred yards of it winding up into the ridges.

He held his steaming horse in the dense cover of *madroñas*. The animal had stopped wheezing by the time Cousin Jack came into view, spurring his stumbling animal into a run. As the Cornishman drew near, he slowed his horse down, obviously looking for Anders on the main trail below.

When the man was fifteen feet away, Anders pulled his horse around till it was pointed toward Cousin Jack. He shouted and whacked the horse on the rump. The animal squealed wildly and bolted directly at the Cornishman.

Cousin Jack's horse, skittish with exhaustion, reared high. Cousin Jack couldn't bring the animal down or get it out of the way in time. Ander's horse veered at the last moment but its shoulder struck the other animal. Cousin Jack's horse was still on its hind legs and the blow made it fall. Jack threw himself clear.

Anders had run into the open, his gun out. But Jack's floundering horse blocked the man off. Anders cut to one side to see him and by that time Cousin Jack was rolling over and pulling his gun.

"Drop it!" Anders shouted. "Jack, I've got a gun on you!"

Lying on his belly, Jack swung his gun up and fired. The bullet went past Anders, who squeezed out one shot in reaction before he could stop himself. If he killed Jack, he'd never find the straps.

He spun and threw himself back into the cover of the *madroñas*. One of the roots caught his foot, tripping him. He pitched headlong beneath the matted growth of the tree. It probably saved his life, for he could hear Jack's bullets crashing through the foliage just above his falling body, but when he hit the ground, the gun was jarred from his hand.

Sprawled across the root system of the twisted tree, Anders saw the Paterson lying in the open, within reach. He grabbed for it. Jack's gun slammed. Anders jerked his hand back as the bullet kicked up dirt an inch beyond his fingers.

Jack's frantic horse had regained its feet and was crashing off into the timber. When the sounds of its passage faded, all Anders could hear was his own breathing. The mass of the tree hid him from Jack. Huddled against its protection, he heard Jack get up. He heard Jack's footsteps coming toward him. He looked up and saw Jack towering over him. Anders rose slowly from behind the tree.

Frostbite had left ugly scabs on the Cornishman's cheeks. He hadn't shaved in days and a bristly black beard joined his ragged side whiskers. He was hatless and his long hair and shaggy coat were matted with dirt and brush.

He emitted the pungent reek of some animal just out of its cave. His eyes had the filmed, red-rimmed look of a man in high fever. Anders stared at them, realizing his life hung on the whim of a crazed mind. The gun in Jack's hand was cocked. Anders was afraid his first word might set it off. Yet he had to try, had to throw Jack off somehow.

"Where are those straps?" he asked abruptly.

The man stared at him blankly. For a moment Anders thought he would not speak. Then the lips moved. "What straps?"

"The connecting straps. The ones you took from Mulligan's forge."

"I didn't take no straps."

"And I suppose you didn't saw the beam."

"Beam?"

"The one Mason went down on."

The gun moved. "Damn you, Anders!"

"Somebody sawed it," Anders said quickly. It checked Jack a moment. Anders saw surprise in the man, confusion, as well as the frustrated rage. It was not the reaction Anders had expected. But it was a genuine reaction. The Cornishman was in no shape to mask his feelings. It took Anders a moment to adjust his own thinking, after his deep suspicions of the man. But the expression on Jack's face finally convinced him. Jack had not known about the sawed beam.

Anders said: "It was a fool thing for me to

do . . . jumping up and down on the beam. But Mason would have gone anyway, the minute he put his weight on it. It wouldn't have carried both of us." Cousin Jack frowned at Anders, like a child trying to concentrate. Anders knew a touch of hope. He said, tensely: "All you have to do is come back to camp with me, Jack. The beam's there."

"All I have to do is kill you," Jack said thickly. "All I have to do is blow your head off."

"It would be like killing Mason all over again," Anders said. "It would be killing his last dream. Do it and the bridge won't be finished. Without the bridge Opal won't have a dime. Could you do that to her?"

Jack swayed, staring intently at him. He blinked his feverish eyes. Anders could almost see the film shredding. When Jack spoke, his voice sounded small, lost.

"Anders . . . the beam . . . was it really sawed?"

"You can see for yourself."

The Cornishman touched his forehead. He looked at the boulder. He looked at the trees. He looked at the ground on either side of him. He made a groaning sound and shut his eyes. He crossed to the boulder and sat down on it. The gun slipped from his fingers. He put his big head in his hands.

"Not real, Anders . . . nothing's real. Am I awake now? A terrible feeling . . . I can't remember . . . I was shooting at you in the rain. Where was that?"

"Never mind," Anders said. "It's over now. Why don't we go back to camp?"

Cousin Jack was more lucid by the time they reached camp. Anders showed him the sawed beam, and then took him to the cook shack and had Tin Pan fix him a meal. The man was ravenous. Anders was convinced now that Cousin Jack had not taken the connecting straps. While the man was eating, Anders went out to find Mulligan. The blacksmith was at the piers. Anders told him they would have to use makeshift straps. Mulligan thought it was impossible.

"There's still iron left in camp," Anders said. "Take the tires and fittings off every wagon. Throw in the cookware, every kettle and frying pan. . . ."

"There still won't be enough."

"Then we'll tie what's left together with cable."

"Wind starts blowin', that wire will pull right out."

"Not if we alternate on the diagonal, cable at one joint, strap at the next. Hop to it, Mulligan."

As the blacksmith left, Anders heard something behind him. It was a group of riders. Two of them had already dismounted: Opal Mason and Jamaica. Jamaica was looking at him intently, and he knew she must have overheard his talk with Mulligan. She wore a heavy cape, the hood over her head. Her cheeks were glowing from the wind and her eyes made a dark and vivid flash in the shadow of the hood.

He felt a chaos of emotion. He couldn't identify it all himself. It had been a shock, seeing her. Yet there was none of the frantic, boyish eagerness he had known when he had first seen her in Hangtown, making him feel so foolish, stumbling over his words, unable to say what he really felt. There was none of the frustration or sense of incompetence he had always known with her. The awkward silence did not disturb him. He could let it run on without embarrassment, waiting for her to speak. It was Jamaica who showed the first tension. A shadowy change of expression ran across her face. Her lips compressed.

"Well," she said, "you have quite a bridge here, Glenn. It was worth the trip."

Victor Castine was helping his wife out of the saddle. Behind them, on big Missouri mules, sat Sluefoot and one of his Pikes. Sluefoot grinned sheepishly and pulled at a pointed ear.

"Mister Castine talked us into it, Anders. With everybody comin' back, we felt like a passel o' varmints scroungin' around the edge o' camp."

"I can use some men that know what to do with a hammer," Anders said. "Those coolies are about to drive me crazy."

"The women insisted on coming," Castine said. "I couldn't hold them back."

"I feel it's my place," Opal said.

Laurette Castine pulled fussily at her fur coat. "Can't we get out of this wind, Victor? It will ruin my complexion."

Jamaica stirred then. Anders thought she was going to speak. She was still watching him and there was a strange look on her face. Before she could say anything, one of the Ducks came off the bridge and stood above Anders on the pier.

"One o' them chinks almost fell off at the end of the flume," he said. "Now he's froze there and we can't get by him."

"Get the company agent out there," Anders said.

"He's been there for fifteen minutes, talkin' to the chink. He can't do nothin'."

Anders nodded at Castine and the women, then climbed onto the pier. The flume was laid on the supporting beams, a wooden canal twenty feet wide with sides six feet high. It was swaying in the wind as Anders followed the trapper out. He could see the two figures in the distance. Just beyond the end of the flume a coolie was sprawled across the naked tie beam. In the flume itself was the company agent, a man named Ah Fong, squatting down and talking with the man.

"*Sun more see*, Paak Suuk," he said. "*Loy che che, yo ho see.*"

The coolie would not answer. He lay rigidly across the tie beam, his eyes shut tight, gripping the truss rods with desperate hands. The whole bridge was swaying in the wind. The coolie's gray rags were whipped about his skinny yellow legs and his face was shiny with strain.

"Tell him I'm here to help," Anders told Ah Fong. "Tell him to relax and we'll get him to safety."

He stepped out on the beam and tried to pry the coolie loose.

"No, no!" Ah Fong cried. "He fight you! You both go fall!"

"It's true," the Duck said. "I tried it with three men and all of us almost went off."

Anders squatted down beside the coolie. He was balanced precariously on the beam and the wind buffeted his body with such force that he could feel his feet keep slipping.

"All right," Anders said, "tell him that, if he falls from here, his bones will never get back to the Flowery Kingdom."

The agent moaned. "Ah, no, I no can say that."

"You've got to. Tell him that he can't hang on forever. His grip will weaken sooner or later and this wind will tear him off. Tell him that if he falls from this height, he'll break into so many pieces we'll never be able to find him."

The agent covered his eyes and made a keening

sound. Then he licked his lips and began to talk with the coolie in Chinese. Anders saw a shudder go through the coolie's body. Anders grabbed an arm. The hand would not release its grip. He made a signal to the Duck, who stepped gingerly onto the beam and got hold of the other arm.

"Keep talking," Anders told Ah Fong. "Drive it home. If he doesn't let us get him to safety, his bones will never get back to China."

The agent repeated what he had said. Another shudder went through the coolie. Anders kept tugging. Finally one hand came loose. All along the flume and out on the naked skeleton of beams the men were fixed in static postures, watching. The Duck pulled. The man's other hand slipped from its hold.

It was like lifting a brittle, contorted mummy back into the flume. The man was in a spasm. Even when he was safe, he would not open his eyes. The muscles of his clenched jaw made hard ridges against the shiny yellow cheeks. Anders and the Duck had to carry him bodily all the way back to the pier.

There was a crowd of Chinese gathered around the pier, piping like birds in their singsong chatter. Anders turned the man over to them. Castine was already taking his wife toward the engineer's shack, but Opal and Jamaica had remained by the pier.

"What on earth did you say to that Chinaman?" Opal asked.

"Something about bones," Anders said, smiling. "Wasn't the trip a little hard on you?" Anders asked Jamaica.

"When I was a little girl on the island," she replied, "I used to ride all day long."

"The wagon road comes quite a bit past the Golden Monte," Opal said. "It left us only half a day in the saddle." She looked very young and very naïve, beside Jamaica. She moistened her lips. "Mister Anders . . . Glenn . . . about Father . . ."

"It was a terrible blow," he said.

"I mean . . . blaming you . . . when Eddie learned the beam had been sawed. . . ."

"He told me. Give him a little time, Opal. He'll understand . . . everything."

"I think he already does, but he's too proud to admit it," she said. They smiled at each other. "Eddie seems to have grown up overnight. I don't think I could have gotten through this without him."

"Maybe this has made us all grow up a little bit," he said. He looked at Jamaica. Someone called to him from the bridge. Anders told the women he had to go. "Tin Pan always has some hot tea in the shack, if you'd like."

Jamaica sent him a long appraising look. "We'll be there," she said. "Get back to your job."

A hundred feet out on the bridge he stopped and looked back. The women were just disappearing into the shack. Sluefoot was unsaddling by the barracks. A wind buffeted the bridge. It made the cable whine mournfully.

XVII

The next morning Anders came awake to the sound of rain. It made a sodden rattle on the roof and he could hear it dripping steadily through cracks in the shakes. He rose and dressed, putting on his hat and coat. He stepped out the door and stood beneath the sheltering eaves.

It was a heavy rain, heavier than the one he had seen at Hangtown. It filled the world with its dull roar and its downpour hid everything behind a shimmering wall. A man came out of that wall, head bent against the rush of water. He stopped under the eaves, stamping mud from his boots. It was Mulligan, the blacksmith.

"My damn' shop is leakin' so bad I can't get my forge fires lighted," he said. He took his hat off, slapping water from it. "I guess it don't matter much anyhow. You won't git them chinks to work today. That coolie freezing on the bridge yesterday scared their pigtails off. You couldn't get 'em to go out on that bridge in this storm if you was Confucius hisself."

265

"They've got to work," Anders said. "This rain might last a week."

He and the smith crossed to the first cabin. Its single window, glassed in with a row of bottles, made a yellow smear of light in the dark rain. A blaze was going in the clay fireplace, spitting and hissing in the water that swept down the chimney. A dozen Chinese were huddled around the hearth, shivering in their thin clothes.

Anders sent Mulligan for the company agent. When he arrived, Anders used him as interpreter to argue with the Chinese. Anders explained how they were working against time. They couldn't just sit around and wait for the storm to stop. He offered the coolies double wages. He got a rope and demonstrated how a safety harness could be rigged. None of it did any good. The thin yellow men sat on their meatless haunches, moaning and murmuring every time a new burst of water came down the chimney.

Anders went to the other cabins, but with each group of Chinese it was the same story. Bribery, threats, logic—none of it would work. By the time he had visited all the cabins he was seething with frustrated anger. He went with Mulligan to the smithy. From wagon tires Mulligan had already forged half a dozen connecting straps. Anders strung them on a line and tied it to his belt. He saw three people wading through the mud from the engineer's shack: Sluefoot, Cousin

Jack, and Opal. The girl had on a heavy cloak, soaked and clinging to her figure. Beneath its hood the edges of her wet hair clung in curling tendrils to her flushed cheeks. She stopped in the dubious shelter of the shack, wiping rain from her eyes.

"You aren't going to go out on that bridge today," she said.

"Them chinks sure ain't," Mulligan said.

"Maybe they'll change their minds when they see somebody out there," Anders said.

Opal frowned at him. "Glenn . . . you?"

He put some tie rods, a dozen nuts and bolts, and a pair of wrenches in a rawhide sack. "Somebody's got to show them it can be done."

"But you can't go out, alone, it's too wet, you'll slip. You can't even see what you're doing."

"Opal, if we had stopped every time something like this happened, you wouldn't even have that cable across the gorge today."

Rain dripped steadily through the roof. Opal wiped it from her face, glancing expectantly at Cousin Jack. He was not looking at her. He was looking at Anders and there was no expression on his face. She turned to Sluefoot.

The Pike shook his head. "I came back to work, Miss Opal, not to commit suicide."

Anders made a disgusted sound. He still had the safety harness he had devised out of rope to demonstrate to the Chinese. He hitched it around his waist, slung the sack of rods and bolts over his shoulder, and started for the bridge.

He heard Opal call something after him, but it was lost in the unremitting roar of the rain. He waded through mud and reached the slippery rock trail to the bridge.

There were only a dozen major beams left to attach. They were heaped on the pier, unpeeled logs fifteen feet long. One was a load for two men, but Anders tilted it onto his shoulder and started out on the bridge.

The rain poured against his face in a blinding torrent. He had to feel his way down the slant of the bridge, hanging onto the side of the flume with one hand. The bottom was slippery. Twice he fell. Once he almost lost the beam overboard. By the time he reached the midway point his hands were bloody and full of splinters.

He struggled to the end of the flume. There was still fifty feet of the structure left to build. The only thing between the end of the flume and the pier on the edge of the cliff was the cable, stretching bare and silvery in the rain. They had been using a rope sling to hang the beams from the cable while they made the permanent attachments. They had rigged a windlass to haul the beam into position. Anders hitched one end of the beam to the sling and began to crank the windlass, inching the beam out along the cable till it was extended its full length, its far end hanging from the cable by the sling, its butt resting on the flume at his feet.

Anders went to his hands and knees, bolting on the connecting strap. The rain pounded against his back and he had to keep wiping his eyes to see. It usually took two men to connect the butt of the new beam, one to hold it while the other bolted on the straps. Anders had to swing the end of the beam off the flume to get it into position. Holding it there, he fumbled to jam the bolt through the strap and into its hole in the beam. The bolt slipped from his wet fingers. He watched it plummet out of sight below. Cursing, he fumbled behind him with one hand, trying to get another bolt from the sack.

His knees slipped on the flume, throwing him off balance. He felt the wet beam sliding from his fingers. He made a frantic effort to recover it. He almost pitched off himself and had to let go of the beam and go to his belly on the boards. Helplessly he watched the beam's butt end swing down and out. At the bottom of its pendulum it pulled free of the sling at the far end and fell into the rain-shimmering darkness below.

Anders crouched at the edge of the flume. He didn't know whether the wet on his face was rain or tears. He might as well face it. One man couldn't do it alone. Only a damned stubborn fool wouldn't admit it. He'd be stupid to go on. He'd done all he could. He didn't owe anybody any more, Opal or Mason or Quill or any of them; he'd given all he had. It would be he that went off the bridge next time, instead of a beam, and he'd be a pig-headed fool to go on.

He got up and felt his way back along the flume. Defeat was like a sickness in him. He felt spent and completely exhausted.

When he reached the pier, he stopped and looked off at camp. He couldn't see anything but rain. He looked down at the pile of sodden beams. He began to curse bitterly. He cursed a long time. Then he stooped and got one of the beams by its end and began dragging it back down the bridge.

He got the beam extended in the sling again. This time he put a hitch on the beam's butt end and made it fast to a truss. It held the beam while he bolted on the connecting strap. Now he had to crawl out the beam to the far end and attach it by truss to the cable. He threw a line over the cable above him and made it fast to his safety harness. Hung all over with trusses and tools and his sack of nuts and bolts, he began the precarious trip out on the beam.

It swung with his weight. His hands slipped on the wet surface and panic gagged him. He went to his belly, hugging the beam like a bear. He knew what that Chinese had felt like yesterday.

He forced himself to go on. He reached the end. He had to stand in the sling to tie the truss to the cable above. His shifting weight made the beam start swinging. He caught the ropes, trying to stop the oscillation. But it was too late. He heard the creak of rending iron at the other end. He knew it was one of Mulligan's makeshift connecting straps coming apart. He saw the far end of the beam tear loose from the bridge and drop down. His end of the beam tilted, pulling free of the sling.

He fell with it. Three feet he fell and then the line on his safety harness jerked him so hard he thought he was cut in two. He hung like a rag doll in the harness, watching the beam turn end over end and disappear in the darkness below him.

He twirled in mid-air. The rain beating against him was the only sound in the world. He tried to climb the rope, but it was so wet that his hands slipped and he kept sliding back down. He tried to swing and slide the rope down the slant of the cable toward the bridge, but he saw the knots begin to give and was afraid to jerk at them any more. He looked at the cable, twenty feet above. He looked at the bridge, fifteen feet away. Now he knew he was a damned fool. The safety harness had saved his life, but he would just have to hang here like a monkey on a string till somebody came out and got him.

He began shouting. But it was like yelling through cotton. The dull roar of rain muffled any sound and he knew his yells didn't carry more than ten or fifteen feet.

He hung there for an endless time. He stared emptily into the blackness below. He was finished. This was the last of it. He knew that. He was through. If he ever got out of this, he would pack his gear and saddle up and leave.

Finally he felt a tremor run through the cable above. He saw shapes on the bridge, two shadows, men. It was Cousin Jack and Sluefoot, carrying a beam on their shoulders. They stopped at the end of the flume, putting the beam down. They wiped rain from their eyes, peering out at Anders. Then Sluefoot began to laugh. He put his hands on his hips and threw back his head and laughed.

"I know some other tricks, too," Anders said. "They'll make your head ache like hell if you don't get a line out here and haul me in."

The men weighted a rope with a connecting strap and swung it out to Anders. On the third toss he caught it, and they hauled him into the bridge. Anders stood on the flume, loosening the safety rope about his waist. He felt as though somebody had been working on his middle with a saw. He looked at the beam they had brought out.

"Sort of a peace offering," Cousin Jack said.

Sluefoot took out his chaw. "I guess I've given you a lot of trouble, Anders. Us Missouri Pikes are slower'n molasses runnin' uphill when it comes to trustin' a stranger. But today, seein' you come out here all alone . . . I guess it cracked the ice. I can't hang back no longer. Just give us the word. We'll finish this bridge."

Anders stared at their faces. He looked down at the beam again. Finally he began to grin. He clapped Cousin Jack on the shoulder.

"You've got the word." He laughed at Sluefoot. "Let's go to work."

It rained for two days and two nights, with the three of them working out on the bridge and Mulligan fighting to keep his forge fires lit back in camp. They ran out of iron for the straps and had to make connections with cable. It was the worst time Anders had put in yet, but he came to have a deep appreciation of the two men with him. Cousin Jack was a skilled mechanic and the connectors he devised with cable were wonders of ingenuity. Sluefoot was worth a whole crew. He had inexhaustible energy and nerves like ice. In the evening, when it grew too dark to see, and Cousin Jack and Anders were crawling around on all fours to keep from falling off the wet flume, Sluefoot would still be hanging out in the safety lines working on the trusses. Anders knew they could never have the done the job without him.

XVIII

On Saturday night they finished the bridge. They had a celebration. Tin Pan baked cakes for the whole crew, and Castine opened some champagne he had brought in anticipation of success. Most of the men got so drunk that Anders had a hard time getting enough guards for the bridge. All the trappers but Quill were on patrol along the flume. Cousin Jack finally agreed to guard the near end of the bridge. Sluefoot and his Pike said they'd stand watch at the far end. Quill and Anders were to spell them at midnight.

Anders had been sharing one room in the engineer's shack with Castine, while the women occupied the other. He had planned to turn in early so he could go on guard at midnight, but he was restless and jumpy. He left Castine playing solitaire at the puncheon table and stepped outside.

The smell of thaw was in the air. The smell of ancient, soggy earth and of wet pine needles and of rocks frozen for half a year. The moon would be up soon but now only a hint of light touched Anders from one of the campfires. He moved idly to a tumbled mass of boulders at the edge of the cañon.

He looked at the creaking bridge, barely visible

in the darkness, and tried to feel some sense of achievement. He knew he should feel it. The job was done. His first bridge. He remembered his father and all the rocks that had been moved. It was like a debt that had been paid at last. But still there was no sense of achievement.

He knew why. It wasn't really finished yet. There were too many questions left unanswered. Cousin Jack, Kettle Corey, Hangtown Charlie. It wasn't over yet.

He looked northeast and thought of Dusty. The man should have reached the head gates today. The rivers were filling and water would be in the upper flume, rushing down on them, ten miles, twenty miles, thirty miles an hour, filling the wooden aqueduct to the brim with the dirty yellow, roiling, débris-filled floods of spring. It would reach the bridge any time now, and when it did, the guards would shoot off their guns and arouse the whole camp to see the fruits of their labors.

He heard a rustle of movement and wheeled quickly, hand going to the holstered Paterson revolver. He could barely make out a cloaked woman's figure, moving through the rocks. She was two feet away before he realized it was Jamaica.

She stopped before him and they looked at each other in silence. He could barely see the shape of her face in the dark. The confused emotion moved through him again. Had he really thought it was over when he walked out on her in Hangtown? At least he had not known such intense confusion then. He had made a simple choice and he had stood by it.

"Is the cable going to work in place of the connecting straps?" she asked.

It surprised him. It took him a moment to realize she was referring to his talk with the blacksmith the other day. "It'll hold," he said.

"You've had a lot of trouble," she said. "Opal was telling me. I didn't realize. . . ."

He looked closely at her face. Her words were brittle, strained, masking something. It wasn't natural that they should stand and talk so casually after all that had happened. Warily he said: "Somebody's trying to stop the bridge. I thought it was Cousin Jack. Now that's canceled out. But there's still this Kettle Corey, from Sacramento Shippers. Do you know anything about him?"

She shook her head. "Not him, exactly. But . . ." She bit her lip, a childish habit she had when she tried to think. "It seems to me . . . Victor said something once in Frisco . . . he mentioned that Sacramento was a subsidiary of the Golden Monte."

"What?" He stared at her, trying to see the implications. "Is there anything else that might have a connection? Can you remember anything they said . . . ?"

She shook her head.

He said: "What's the story on Laurette? I've always had a feeling . . . something there . . . she isn't as sick as she'd like people to believe. Is she really the power behind the throne?"

"I hadn't thought of it. She treats Victor like a little boy. She's a strange woman."

"And jealous as hell," Anders said. "She was ready to stick a knife in Victor at the party. A woman like that . . . making this kind of a trip . . . she must be deathly afraid of you and Victor."

She did not answer. She changed the subject abruptly. "That was quite a thing," she said. "That Chinaman on the bridge . . . even his own people unable to get him off."

"Part of the business."

"A business you really know, Glenn. I never saw you at your work. In all the time we were married I never saw you doing your job. You're good, Glenn. It's what Innes was talking about, isn't it? The genuine people, the real talents . . . when you see them at their work, you know it."

She was speaking more swiftly now, a little breathlessly. It was beginning to come out, the brittle, emotional thing he had sensed behind her casual talk.

"Innes was right, wasn't he?" she said. "The spark . . . I never had it. The theater, they always knew, even if they didn't say it. In New Orleans they knew. In New York. I didn't belong. I wouldn't admit it . . . maybe that was part of the perpetual act, I don't know . . . but when I heard Innes put it into words . . ."

"He was drunk."

"It didn't matter. I felt toward him as I did toward Booth. If Booth had told me the truth in the beginning, I would have quit."

Her voice was growing shrill, a little frantic. He hadn't realized how deeply that evening at the hotel had shaken her.

"Are you saying you want to give it up?" he asked.

"Why do you think I came here?" she said. "I had to see you, Glenn. . . ." She put her hands on his shoulders, gripping tight. She moved against him. "You came to this country to take me back, Glenn. I'll go now."

He had spent two years dreaming of this moment. He had traveled ten thousand miles to hear her say these words.

"I've got to finish the bridge first," he said.

"Oh, Glenn, what does the bridge matter now? We're together. We can go back . . . New Orleans, New York, where we belong."

He thought about the Chinese cook, with his tongue cut out, who had shinnied down the beam to save Anders when nobody else was willing to risk his life. He thought about Barton, who stood to lose the stake that would bring his family west, if the bridge didn't get finished. And Quill,

278

who'd have to go back to standing hip-deep in the icy mountain streams. "Jamaica, I wish I could explain . . ."

"What's there to explain?"

He looked at her. He knew she was right. He could not explain it to her. She must have seen some of it in his face.

"Do you remember what you said when you first found me in Hangtown?" she asked. "You'd do anything to get me back. *Anyway you want it,* you said, *anything you want.* Well, this is how I want it. If you want me back, we'll leave now."

Her head was tilted at the calculated angle, her eyes flashing. Or was it calculated any more? Maybe she had done it for so many years that it was no longer an affectation. He wondered why it didn't irritate him. He couldn't feel anything. She looked so different to him now. He couldn't feel any irritation or anger or excitement or even pity. Something had died in him. Maybe it had been dying, bit by bit, ever since their first reunion in Hangtown. Or maybe it had started when she slapped Innes. Or when he kissed Opal. . . .

He said: "I think, if you'd waited for the bridge to be finished, I would have gone with you. I would have been convinced that you'd really changed."

"Glenn, I have, I've seen the truth about myself. . . ."

"Are you afraid, Jamaica?" he asked. The

way she pulled back, he knew he had struck something. He said: "I don't think it's the truth Innes gave you so much as humiliation. And you can't go back and face the players after that. Always before there were a dozen men waiting to take you off my hands. Now there's nobody. Not even Victor."

"Do you think I couldn't have him? One word, all it would take is one word. . . ."

"I don't think so."

Anger made her face ugly. In a childish defiance, she said: "Do you want me to show you?"

He wasn't going to answer. Then a thought struck him. He remembered what Jamaica had told him—Laurette, the power behind the throne, Sacramento Shippers. He thought of hell and the fury of a woman scorned. He wondered just how infuriated Laurette would be, if she found her man in another woman's arms.

He smiled crookedly at Jamaica. "I'll send him out."

He left her, walking to the engineer's shack. He was filled with a sense of release. He wondered if there would be regrets later on. He couldn't tell. Now he only knew that it was over. The wind blew against him, sharp and clear, carrying the smell of new spring grass.

He went into the engineer's shack. Tin Pan was stoking the fire and Castine sat at the table with his cards. He looked up with a knowing smile. He brushed the white streak in his black hair with one finger.

"Laurette asleep?" Anders asked idly.

"She retired some time ago," Castine said. "Another little spat?"

Anders knew he was referring to Jamaica. Anders was sorry for his inspiration of a few moments ago. He didn't want to send Castine out there. It seemed wrong, to use Jamaica in such a game. He didn't have enough to go on. It would be a gesture of spite, or revenge. "You don't fight any more when it's all over, Victor," he said.

Castine shuffled the cards together and put them down. He thought he would take a smoke, he said.

Anders watched him go out the door. When it was shut, Anders walked to the fireplace. He heard a sound and turned to see that Laurette had appeared at the door of the room the women were occupying. She looked at the front door, her face pinched and vicious. She went back into the room, and, when she reappeared, she had on her heavy cape over her night dress, and the inevitable reticule clutched in both hands. She went out the door with hardly a glance at Anders.

He hesitated. Without intending to, he had started the wheels rolling. He had no more control of it now, and he might as well take advantage of the opportunity.

He went outside.

Nobody was in sight. At first all he could hear was the bridge creaking in the wind. He moved toward the rocks. He could not see anybody but finally he could hear the voices. Laurette's shrill, vindictive tones: "All these years . . . this pretense . . . you're a child, Victor, a little child. I was nothing more than a purse to you, was I? And now the purse is empty . . . you're getting out."

"Laurette, you're wrong."

"I know what's in your mind, Victor. Sell out, get away with her. I was a fool to think she wasn't any different from the others. It won't do you any good, Victor. That Chinaman is too smart for you."

"He didn't see the mine," Victor said. "We didn't let him get near. . . ."

"Don't you think he's guessed? A pig in a poke . . ."

"Laurette, watch your tongue."

"I've watched it long enough."

Laurette heard Anders coming through the rocks and whirled. She had a top-snap pepperbox gripped in her bony fist. It was not over two inches long, and must have come from her gaping reticule. Jamaica was standing to one side, biting her lips, listening to the Castines argue, her eyes wide.

"A pig in a poke?" Anders said. "Is the vein

pinched out? Is that why the Golden Monte had a cave-in?"

"Anders," Castine said, "she's crazy. Don't listen to her."

"I don't have to," Anders said. "I can figure it out from here myself. Your mine was pinching out, both the quartz and the hydraulicking. You could keep people out of the shafts with that cave-in. But if this water came through and you didn't start hydraulicking again, your buyer would get suspicious. And if you did start placering, they would see there wasn't any color in those sluices. You were trying to unload on the Chinese before that happened. You almost made it, Castine. Kong Chow was so eager to get into a big operation they might have bought the Golden Monte on its reputation alone. If this water hadn't come through."

"It hasn't come through yet," Laurette said.

Anders saw that she was looking at the bridge. He couldn't be sure but he thought he saw a tiny flicker of light at the far end. His reaction was automatic. Forgetting the gun, forgetting everything else, he started for the bridge.

"Laurette!" Victor called. "Stop him!"

"Stop *him?*" she cried. Her voice was shrill and cracked with all the unsupportable jealousy he had seen in her face at the party. The pepperbox made a coughing sound. Anders saw Castine spin halfway around, clap a hand to one shoulder, and then sit down. Jamaica uttered a cry, started toward Castine, then whirled and ran toward the shack.

Laurette was still turned toward Castine, her face twisted into something diabolic. Anders lunged at her. She tried to wheel but he reached her too soon, knocking the gun from her hand with a blow on the arm. He kicked it over the edge of the cliff, then turned and ran up the trail.

He reached the pier, calling for the guards. There was no answer. He climbed onto the pier and almost stumbled over a man. It was Cousin Jack, unconscious. Jack must have known who-ever it was that hit him. He wouldn't have let him get close enough otherwise. Anders went to one knee, shaking him.

"Jack . . . who was it? Is he out on the bridge?"

The man groaned feebly, starting to come around. Anders could not wait. He rose and ran onto the bridge. He knew the light was no illusion now. He could see it flickering again at the far edge.

The span yawed in the wind. He knew he was halfway across when he reached the bottom of the dip and started on an upward slant, He was shaken and battered from being thrown against the sides by the constant sway and pitch of the bridge. He was winded and panting heavily but the sounds he made were drowned in the booming racket of the wind, the whine of the cable and rods, the creak of strained joints in the framework.

He saw the light again, a larger flare. It made a yellow bloom against the three men on the pier. One was standing, a massive, unmistakable shape—Kettle Corey. The other two were crouched down, fighting to shield a match from the wind. It flared against their faces. Anders recognized Sluefoot and the other Missouri Pike who had come with him.

The match went out. He heard Sluefoot curse. Until now the wind and the noise of the bridge had covered their sounds as well as his. But they must have become aware of the steady slam of his feet, a more regular pattern than the buffeting of the wind.

Sluefoot pulled his gun as he rose. His first bullet ricocheted off a tie rod with a tortured scream. Anders had his Paterson out. They were both shooting wildly, in the darkness, on the swaying bridge. Anders used Sluefoot's flashes for his target. On his second shot Anders saw the other Pike turn in panic, run across the pier, and jump off. Anders's fourth shot struck Sluefoot and knocked him back onto the pier, where he rolled off onto the ground.

Kettle Corey was shooting now, too. But he was no gunman. Anders could hardly see the man. Still running, he fired two shots without hitting anything. The teamster didn't do any better. Anders made no target, veering back and forth on the yawing bridge. Corey's bullets made a wild spray around him, cracking through the wood, screaming off iron.

When the gun was empty, he threw it at Anders. The engineer dodged blindly. Kettle came down the steep slant of the bridge like a charging bull.

Three hundred pounds of beef and bone crashed into Anders. It knocked him from his feet and Kettle went with him. Anders was underneath, driven against the bridge with stunning impact by the immense weight on top of him.

There was a deafening roar in his head and he thought it was from the fall. He barely heard Kettle wheeze. He felt the man roll off, and then he was grasped beneath the arms. He struggled feebly, slamming a weak blow at the man's face. But he was still dazed from the fall.

He felt himself lifted onto the side of the flume, hanging there like a sack of meal, head outside, feet inside. He caught a tie rod in his left hand, fighting to keep the man from pushing him over. He thought of Garrett Mason, spinning as he fell.

Then Kettle Corey grunted sickly and his clawing weight was gone. Clutching the tie rod, struggling to shift his balance back inside the flume, Anders saw that Corey was struggling with another man. A great, bear-like figure in a shaggy fur coat. It was Cousin Jack.

The Cornishman's first blow had torn Corey

away from Anders. His second blow knocked Corey backward. The teamster checked himself and met Jack's rush. They grappled and their violent struggle carried them stumbling backward down the slant of the flume.

Anders was lowering himself off the side into the flume when he felt it begin to shake. He heard a roaring sound in the distance. He knew what it was and he clawed his way back into the tie rods.

"Jack!" he shouted. "The water!"

The black rush of water came out of the darkness. The flume was shuddering so violently it almost shook Anders off. Kettle and Jack were still fighting when the flood struck them. They were torn apart like rag dolls, lifted upward, helpless in the swollen river of mud and water and débris. Kettle swept by Anders first. All Anders could see were his arms and legs flailing helplessly. One of them caught on a truss and it made a fulcrum. The churning water tipped him over the side and he was gone.

The Cornishman came right behind him. Hanging onto the trusses, Anders swung both legs toward the man, into the irresistible rush.

"Jack!" he screamed.

One of his boots hit the Cornishman's head. Cousin Jack flailed wildly, wrapping both arms about Anders's leg. It almost pulled Anders's arms from their sockets. He shouted with the pain. But he kept his grip. The deluge swept Jack against the inside of the flume. He managed to hook a leg over the side. With one hand he released Anders's leg, clutching for a tie rod. Choking, coughing, spewing, he pulled himself blindly up out of the water.

Dripping and half-drowned, they hung in the trusses till they recovered their strength. Finally, struggling to keep their feet above the boiling current, working hand over hand along the chill cable, they made their way through the trusses to the pier. Anders climbed off the pier and stood with his back against it, weak and trembling. Jack came down beside him, sliding to a sitting position.

"A vote of thanks, Anders," he said feebly.

"I guess the score's about even," Anders said.

Sluefoot lay on the ground where he had fallen, blood still pumping out of his thigh. Anders took off his belt to make a tourniquet that would stop the bleeding.

"Let him be," Jack said.

"I can't do that."

"He's the one that sawed the beam, ain't he? He killed Mister Mason."

"I guess so," Anders said. "That act in the rain . . . working on the bridge these last two days . . . it was just so I'd trust him enough to let him guard the bridge. Is that right, Sluefoot?"

The Pike was only half-conscious. He stared up

at Anders, his eyes filmed with shock and pain. Anders tightened the tourniquet.

"You might as well talk," Anders said. "The water's on its way. The whole Mother Lode will know the story as soon as the water reaches the Golden Monte."

"The Golden Monte?" Jack said. "What's that got to do with it?"

Anders looked at Sluefoot, waiting for the man to confirm what he had only guessed at so far. Sluefoot groaned.

"The Castines were trying to stop the bridge from going through," Sluefoot said. "There's nothing left in the Golden Monte. It pinched out. If the water reached them, there was no way they could keep the fact a secret. They wanted to sell the mine to the Chinese first. . . ."

"A mine that rich?" Jack shook his head. "If it *was* pinched out . . . how could they keep it quiet?"

"They discovered it at the end of the season," Sluefoot said. "Most of the crew had already left. There's only a skeleton crew at the mine now. The Castines kept them quiet with a promise of sharing in the sale. Kettle Corey was cut in when they got him to try and stop Anders on the Downieville road."

"And you were working for the Castines from the beginning," Anders said to Sluefoot. "All that sabotage . . . you pushed that good-luck rock

289

down on me the first time I came here, the flume blown up, the stolen connecting rods . . . it was all you."

Sluefoot closed his eyes, nodding weakly. Cousin Jack stared emptily at the wounded Pike.

"It don't make sense," Jack said. "I wanted to kill you for Mister Mason, Anders . . . and it should have been this one I wanted to kill, all along . . . and now I don't want to do anything. It's all gone, there's nothing more left in me."

Anders got to his feet, putting a hand on Jack's shoulder. Tiredly he said: "Stay here and watch Sluefoot, will you? I'll send some men to carry him back."

Anders could see torches blinking on the trail that slanted down the opposite face of the gorge. In the pale moonlight he could see a shadowy figure far ahead of the lowest torch. He didn't realize that it was a woman until he reached the foot of the trail on his side. Then he saw her hurrying across the narrow, rocky bottom of the cañon. She called his name. It was Opal's voice.

They met in the boulder-strewn sand. He took her in his arms and held her tight. She didn't have to say anything. Her lips on his told it all.

He had come out here to find a woman. He had found her.

ADDITIONAL COPYRIGHT INFORMATION

ABOUT THE AUTHOR

Les Savage, Jr. was born in Alhambra, California and grew up in Los Angeles. His first published story was "Bullets and Bullwhips" accepted by the prestigious magazine, Street & Smith's *Western Story*. Almost ninety more magazine stories followed, all set on the American frontier, many of them published in Fiction House magazines such as *Frontier Stories* and *Lariat Story Magazine* where Savage became a superstar with his name on many covers. His first novel, *Treasure of the Brasada*, appeared from Simon & Schuster in 1947. Due to his preference for historical accuracy, Savage often ran into problems with book editors in the 1950s who were concerned about marriages between his protagonists and women of different races—a commonplace on the real frontier but not in much Western fiction in that decade. Savage died young, at thirty-five, from complications arising out of hereditary diabetes and elevated cholesterol. However, as a result of the censorship imposed on many of his works, only now are they being fully restored by returning to the author's original manuscripts. Among Savage's finest Western stories are *Fire Dance at Spider Rock* (Five Star Westerns, 1995), *Medicine Wheel*

(Five Star Westerns, 1996), *Coffin Gap* (Five Star Westerns, 1997), *Phantoms in the Night* (Five Star Westerns, 1998), *The Bloody Quarter* (Five Star Westerns, 1999), *In The Land of Little Sticks* (Five Star Westerns, 2000), *The Cavan Breed* (Five Star Westerns, 2001), *Danger Rides the River* (Five Star Westerns, 2002), and *Black Rock Cañon* (Five Star Westerns, 2006). Much as Stephen Crane before him, while he wrote, the shadow of his imminent death grew longer and longer across his young life, and he knew that, if he was going to do it at all, he would have to do it quickly. He did it well, and, now that his novels and stories are being restored to what he had intended them to be, his achievement irradiated by his powerful and profoundly sensitive imagination will be with us always, as he had wanted it to be, as he had so rushed against time and mortality that it might be.

Books are produced in the United States using U.S.-based materials

Books are printed using a revolutionary new process called THINKtech™ that lowers energy usage by 70% and increases overall quality

Books are durable and flexible because of smythe-sewing

Paper is sourced using environmentally responsible foresting methods and the paper is acid-free

Center Point Large Print
600 Brooks Road / PO Box 1
Thorndike, ME 04986-0001 USA

(207) 568-3717

US & Canada:
1 800 929-9108
www.centerpointlargeprint.com